EARTHQUAKES

To Avery, thanks for letting your mona read the book.

06-08-24

Sarah Maury Swan

Sarah Maury Swan

Earthquakes

ISBN 978-1-7345094-0-3

Chapter 1

JONATHON COULDN'T DECIDE WHETHER real earthquakes or his recurring earthquake nightmare scared him more, but he sure wished they would both go away. He patted Mary Anne's shoulder as his sister shook beside him in the threshold to his bedroom. He wanted to shiver too, but that wouldn't be manly enough. The ground was not just trembling beneath them, he thought he could feel the floor boards in their house heaving.

Jonathon suppressed a sigh. *Why he was always the one the family came to for comfort. Especially now that they were in a war against Japan and Germany.*

Ever since their dad went to the Philippines a month after Japan blew up Pearl Harbor, the whole family seemed to be in silent mode. As if waiting for more bad things to happen.

And now Los Angeles was earthquake central. At least that's the way it felt to Jonathon. It was only September and already they'd had three big 'quakes, including a one powerful enough to knock down the tree in front of their house and make a miniature mountain range out of the sidewalk. The good news was that the tree had not taken their roof out.

"Jonathon? Do you think Mom's scared, like us?" Mary Anne tilted her head back as she looked up.

"I guess so. Why do you ask?"

"Well, ever since we heard that the Philippines were attacked, it's almost as if she thinks everything's just hunky dory."

Jonathon patted his sister's arm. "I heard on the radio that we all had to be calm. To not show our fear. Maybe that's what Mom's doing."

The floor stopped jerking and the rumbling outside quit. Mom called from downstairs. "Mary Anne? Jonathon? You two okay up there?"

Jonathon called out, "We're fine. How's everybody downstairs?"

"We're fine as well," called Mom.

"We only lost one dish this time," yelled Mary Anne's twin, Christopher.

Jonathon's older brother, Richard, laughed and said, "There's still enough water in the pond for the goldfish, so this one wasn't as bad as the others."

Jonathon wondered if his older brother would restart the morning argument with Mom now that the earthquake was over. Jonathon wasn't sure why Richard kept fighting with Mom when he knew she didn't want him to quit college and enlist. *He's already twenty-one, why doesn't he just go?*

He gave Mary Anne's shoulder on final squeeze and turned back into his bedroom. "I've got to finish getting ready for school, Sis. I'll see you downstairs."

After she was gone, Jonathon shut the door and shook. He needed to get rid of his own feelings of dread. It was bad enough to dream about 'quakes, but real ones scared him close to senseless. It was almost guaranteed he'd have a nightmare tonight. He wished they still lived in New Bern, North Carolina. Hurricanes were much easier to deal with.

Rising voices from the kitchen below him made his shoulders' sag. He sighed and finished putting fresh shiny pennies in his loafers before slipping his feet into them. Richard wasn't done with the argument. Jonathon thought he'd better get down there before his brother started pounding the table again.

It would be nice to just hide and not worry about other people in his family. Maybe because he was bigger and stronger than his brothers, he was supposed to take care of them. But he was only seventeen. Couldn't tell Richard what to do. Couldn't tell Mom what to do. He wished they could just come to some kind of agreement.

Jonathon headed down the stairs, but just before he got to the kitchen, Richard, snorting like a charging bull, slammed into him.

"Sorry, Jonathon," Richard said, taking a step back. "Mom was worse than ever today. She just won't listen." He laid his hands on Jonathon's shoulders. "See if you can talk sense into her."

Jonathon stepped back and shook his head. "I don't want you to go either, Richard. You gotta understand that. But I know you think it's important. That you're letting our country down. That you're not doing your part."

Richard nodded and opened his mouth to speak.

But Jonathon held up his hand. "Let me finish."

Richard stepped back a pace and punched one fist into his other palm.

"Try looking at it from Mom's side. She scared to death the Navy's going to knock on the door and tell her Dad's missing, or dead in a battle. Or Granddaddy. Or both of them. I'm betting she doesn't want to worry about her children as well."

"What do you..." Richard said.

Jonathon shook his head. "I'm not done here. Look at the good you'd do if you finished studying cryptology in college. Maybe you'd break the enemies' codes. You've only got a semester left."

"You're no help," Richard snarled. He pulled papers out of his pants pocket and waved them in his brother's face. "I am enlisting today."

Jonathon shrugged his shoulders. "If that's what you think is best. Hope you kill those Japs everywhere you see them." He patted his brother's shoulder. "But just remember how to duck."

Chapter 2

WHEN JONATHON WALKED INTO the kitchen Mom was wiping her face with a tissue, but she smiled and said, "Good morning, darling, you barely have time for breakfast. Shall I scramble from eggs for you?"

"I'll just have toast. I don't want to be late. Besides, Christopher and Mary Anne are waiting for me." He gave his mother a peck on her cheek. "Are you going to be home when we get back from school?"

His mother grinned, "I'm doing late shift today and we're having a pot roast for dinner to celebrate our being together."

Jonathon's mouth dropped open in surprise. "How'd you get the rations for a roast?"

"A friend's going out of town and didn't want to waste her rations."

Jonathon smeared jelly on his toast and waved goodbye. "See you tonight."

When he came out the front door, Mary Anne and Christopher started down the street, but stopped behind a grey car parked in front of their neighbor, Dr. Ringwaldt's, garage.

"What a weird looking car," said Christopher.

"Yeah," said Mary Anne, "is it coming or going?"

"That's the new Studebaker model, I think," said Jonathon. "Wonder how Dr. Ringwaldt could afford a new car.

"Yeah," said Christopher, "they went up in price after the factories were ordered not to make any more last February."

"And how come he didn't park it in his garage," Mary Anne added. "He's always so careful."

But before either of the twins could answer, a low-flying plane caught their attention. Could be a Zero come to strafe the town, or it could a Japanese bomber about to do damage. Jonathon visualized a flattened L.A.

As the plane flew over, Christopher, the family plane expert, pumped his fist in the air. "That's the new American B-17 Lockheed developed. Probably out for a test flight."

"Wonder if Mom worked on it," said Mary Anne, waving at the pilot.

Down the street, their friends beckoned them to hurry up. The first bell from school shrilled, urging them into jog.

"I'll meet you at home after school. I've got track practice until 4. Learn lots today." Jonathon headed off to where his friends were standing.

"Hey Jennifer, did you see that plane? It was a B-17, wasn't it?" Jonathon circled his arm around his girlfriend's waist

Jennifer smiled her brilliant smile at him and flattened him with her sparkling chocolate-brown eyes. "I think my brother Michael worked on that one. If I remember correctly, it had the same insignia letters on the tail."

Seeing Jennifer reminded Jonathon of the new car in Dr. Ringwaldt's driveway. Her parents were good friends with him. "Did Dr. R get a new car, Jennifer? The twins and I saw one at his house this morning."

"Don't know about that, but Dad said he's out of town."

Jonathon held the school's front door open. "Why would a strange car be in his driveway?"

But just as they reached the seniors' lockers, the second bell rang. She shrugged and waved goodbye, her glossy, black hair shimmering around her shoulders. "See you at lunch?"

Jonathon nodded at her back and called, "Sure." He grabbed his math and history books out of his locker on his way to homeroom, slipping into his seat just as the third bell rang.

While Mrs. Reid called roll, Jonathon slid out his math homework and finished the last problem. Then he pulled out his history book to read the last page on the Greek Empire. He knew he should have taken the books home with him, but hadn't had time yesterday. Besides, what else was homeroom for?

The school's P.A. system squawked, signaling the beginning of Morning Announcements and Jonathon rose with his classmates to recite the Pledge of Allegiance, hand over his heart and eyes on the flag hanging over the blackboard at the front of the room. After the morning prayer, Vice Principal James Hughes cleared his throat and rustled some papers. He stuttered as he announced a special school-wide assembly to be held instead of third period.

Jonathon thought the man sounded nervous.

Chapter 3

YES! THOUGHT JONATHON, NO boring Latin today. But considering what was going on in the world, maybe boring was good. He wasn't thrilled with the idea of the Nazis or the Japs invading the U.S. He really didn't want to even think about that, but it could happen.

He caught up with his friend Bob who was headed toward their history class, "Any idea what this assembly is about? You worked in the office this morning, didn't you?"

Bob shook his head. "All I know is some fellow in a black suit came in and was immediately pulled into the Principal Robinson's office. Mr. Hughes and a couple of teachers were there also. They all looked as if the Japs had bombed Pearl Harbor again."

"Geeze," muttered Jonathon. "I hope not." *What if the Japs had bombed Pearl Harbor again? Was there anything left of the base to bomb? What about all the natives? Were they safe?*

The first two classes of the day dragged on for what seemed like hours. Even the teachers didn't seem motivated to teach. Everyone was just waiting for whatever the assembly was about.

The minute the bell rang for the end of second period, it was as if the starting gun had gone off to begin a race. Jonathon was the third person out the door. Within a minute his brother appeared beside him.

"What's going on, Jonathon?" Christopher asked.

Jonathon jumped and thumped his hand on his brother's shoulder. "Don't sneak up on a guy like that. I'm almost jumped out my skin."

His brother shrugged.

"Maybe the war has ended," said Mary Anne, grabbing Jonathon's hand and stepping so close to him, she almost tripped him.

"Geeze, Mary Anne, gimme some room here. I do need to walk on my own."

At his sister's sudden down turn of her mouth, Jonathon said, "It'd be nice if the war was over, but I doubt that's happened." Then he turned to whoever was touching his arm. Felt like Jennifer's hand. Yep, the girl always showed up at the right time. Made him feel better, more relaxed and confident that things would turn out well. He smiled at her and slipped his hand around hers.

But next to her was a guy who seemed to be trying to move her away from Jonathon. "Hey Kurt. Haven't seen you for a while. How have you been?"

Kurt nodded at Jonathon and again tried to come between him and Jennifer.

But she slid her fingers between Jonathon's, squeezed lightly and moved closer to him. "I heard the War Department broke up spy ring here in L.A."

"That's creepy," said Christopher, his voice ending in a squeak.

Kurt's eyes sparked with what looked like fear to Jonathon. "When?" he asked.

"I don't know. It's just what I heard." Jennifer said with a shrug.

Jonathon's shoulders tightened even more. Why did he suddenly feel the car at his neighbor's house might be involved? Surely Dr. Ringwaldt wasn't spying for the Germans.

Jonathon was glad they'd reached the auditorium and Mary Anne moved away. Sometimes it would be nice if he didn't have to deal with everyone's problems. Sometimes it would be good to just focus on things like his relationship with Jennifer.

He knew it was tough on Mom, with Dad gone and her having to work to support them.

But why was he the one dealing with the problems? He missed his sister Caroline. Still the problem solver in their family was undoubtedly doing a wonderful job as a nurse in Guam.

When they were all seated and Principal Robinson was standing at the podium, Jonathon sat on the edge of his seat wishing everybody would hush so they could hear what was going on. He glared at the noisy students around him, willing them to pay attention.

Finally, Principal Robinson tapped the microphone to quiet the students. "I know all of you are wondering why I asked you to come. And I wish I had better news to share. I know you were hoping I was going to tell you the war was over."

Students shifted in their seats and some whispered to their neighbors. "Shoot," said the junior sitting on the other side of Jennifer. "I want my dad to come home."

"Don't we all," muttered Jonathon.

The principal tapped the microphone again and said, "Settle down, settle down." When the crowd was quiet again, he said, "The War Department and other government agencies have uncovered a group of Germans who are secretly trying to take down our government."

Again, the students filled the air with questions and comments. The room grew noisier and noisier.

Jonathon immediately thought about the strange car he'd seen. He wondered if his family was safe where they lived. But would they be safe anywhere?

This time it took the principal's banging the gavel on the podium to restore quiet in the room. "I know," he said. "I know you're wondering what you should do and why it's your problem to solve."

The students all nodded and a sophomore sitting in front of Jonathon muttered, "Just what I was wondering. How could I tell a spy from anybody else?"

"Yeah, they're not going slap name tags on saying, 'Hey you, look at me. I'm a spy!'" said his buddy.

"So," started Principal Robinson, not even waiting for the noise to die down, "What we want you to do is just pay attention to what's going on around you. Have you seen anything unusual on your street? A person wandering around you've not seen before. Maybe a strange car..."

Jonathon didn't hear any more of what was being said. Other than the Studebaker, what else had he noticed? Surely Dr. Ringwaldt wasn't a spy. He was a nice guy. Would he really talk baseball with the boy next door, if he was a spy? Maybe, as a ruse. Shaking his head to chase the ugly thoughts out, Jonathon remember walking with his neighbor to distribute tangerines and other fruit from his trees to anybody who looked like he could use some food. Spies didn't do that, did they? Again, maybe.

Jonathon decided to wait and see what was going on with the Studebaker. Probably just someone visiting. Yeah, but what if the visitor was a spy? Wait, hadn't Jennifer said Dr. Ringwaldt out of town? Still, maybe somebody was house-sitting. And was the visitor planning to kill everybody on their street?

And what could Jonathon do to stop him?

Jennifer tickling his arm jerked him back to the present. "What?" he asked. Then he looked around and saw everybody standing up.

"Did you fall asleep, Jonathon?" Jennifer asked. "Did you hear what we're supposed to do if we spot trouble?"

"Yes, but what do they mean by trouble? How can I tell if something is suspicious? Christopher, Mary Anne and I saw a new Studebaker parked in Dr. Ringwaldt's driveway this morning."

"He probably bought a new car."

"See? That's what I mean. How can we tell?" Jonathon kissed Jennifer on the cheek. "See you at lunch."

Chapter 4

JONATHON JUMPED AND LOOKED down when something next to him exploded. *Holy Cow, he was in chemistry class! One of his favorite subjects. What happened to the rest of the day?*

"Jonathon? Is it possible for you to pay attention to the Bunsen burner in front of you before Samantha blows up the lab?" asked his teacher, Mr. Smith. "I gave you two the powdered potassium to work with because I thought you'd do the experiment with her help."

"Sorry, sir," mumbled Jonathon.

Samantha, his lab partner, poked him in the ribs. "I don't know what's happening to you, Jonathon, but I can't do this experiment by myself. I've already made one big mistake."

"What happened?"

"I don't know. The potassium exploded while I was pouring it into the beaker. It isn't supposed to do that, is it?

Jonathon read the instructions. "Oh, yeah. I'm sorry Sammy, I'll take over from here. Potassium is very prone to blowing up if you're not extra careful."

Samantha read the instructions again. "Oh yeah." She pointed to where it said just that in the instructions.

Jonathon took the book from her hands and said, "Let's start over and see if we can do it without blowing up anything else." He patted Sammy's shoulder and stretched his neck from side to side, wishing he could figure out how to get rid of his tension. "I'll handle the powder. You control the temperature."

His mind kept wandering back to what was said during the assembly, but, each time, he caught himself and stared at the powder. He scooped the potassium into a half cup measure inside the container, carefully not exposing the powder to anymore air than he could help. Then, still inside the bag, he held the beaker over the cup and tilted the two upright. He held them together until the beaker was safely on the lit Bunsen Burner.

"Quick, Sammy, seal that bag."

She rushed to grab the bag, but Jonathon held up a hand. "Slow and steady wins the day, here, my friend."

As she sealed the bag, he checked the flame on the burner. "Good, you set this on low."

They heated the powder until it liquified, and then slowly added vinegar. It hissed and bubbled and then it turned into translucent amber-colored beads.

"Wow," said Samantha, "I could make jewelry with these."

Mr. Smith came back around. "And what did you learn, Samantha?

"Um, read the instructions carefully? And I think I know why I don't cook well."

"Why's that?" asked Jonathon.

"My dad says, 'Think before you act, Samantha.' But I don't."

"Keep working at it, Sammy. It'll get easier," Jonathon said patting her shoulder.

Mr. Smith asked, "And what did you learn, Jonathon?"

"I don't know. Um, two chemicals together can change properties when mixed?"

"You are your mother's son, aren't you my boy? What did the heat do to the mixture?"

Samantha answered, "Made it easier for the chemicals to blend?"

"Excellent," said their teacher. "And, yes, you can string the beads together to make jewelry. But they are fragile, so be careful."

When their teacher moved on to the next Bunsen burner, Jonathon said, "Guess we'd better clean up. How about you write up our results and I'll do clean up."

"Thanks, Jonathon. I'll put in the failed attempt and the success."

"Good thinking." He turned off the burner and grabbed the beaker. Crash went the still hot beaker.

"Ow!" yelled Jonathon, and stuck his hand under cold water in the sink. "Talk about acting before thinking, that was just plain stupid."

"What's with you today, Jonathon? You could have really hurt yourself," Samantha turned his hand over to see how bad the burn was. "Not too bad."

"I guess I'm still thinking about Principal R's announcement this morning."

"That's been bothering you all day?"

"Guess so. I don't remember the rest of the day until we were working on this experiment." He got a whisk broom and dustpan from the cleaning-equipment closet.

"I don't want go around thinking everybody's a spy if he's doing something different. And what's different mean?"

Samantha shrugged her shoulders and handed the report to Jonathon to sign. "I don't know, maybe somebody home from work in the middle of the day."

"Mom's home in the middle of the day sometimes. Does that make her a suspect?"

"Everybody knows your mom works different shifts."

"What if she has visitors come to the house for a meeting? Are people going to think she's having a group over to plan the ruin of our country?"

He checked his hand and took a final wipe over the countertop. "It's so confusing. I'm going to think the best of people until proven otherwise."

Samantha patted his arm. "I hadn't thought of all that. And we're just teenagers. Nobody's going to take us seriously."

"Thanks for listening, Sammy. You're a good pal."

The bell rang signaling the end of class and the end of the school day. "See you Monday, Jonathon. And don't worry so much. Everything will be fine."

"I'd like to think you're right. Hey! Aren't you and Eddie going to the movies with Jennifer and me tomorrow?"

"He didn't tell you? I broke up with him yesterday."

Chapter 5

"WHAT? WHY? I THOUGHT you two would never leave each other. I was planning to come to your wedding. Maybe be Eddie's best man."

"Ask him," said Samantha and turned her back.

Jonathon thought he heard her sniff and her wipe hand across her face.

"Bye," she mumbled.

Jonathon watched her leave the room feeling helpless to do anything. He hurried to his locker for his gym clothes. Track practice always lifted his spirits just from the adrenaline rush that running gave him.

When he reached the locker room, Eddie was tying his track shoes on. "Sammy told me you guys broke up? What happened?"

"Beats me. One minute we're fine and the next minute she's cold as ice. Said I told her something that scared her."

Coach Bellows hollered from the doorway, "Let's hustle there you two, time's awasting."

"Call me tonight," Jonathon said, as they walked out the track. "Or come with me for a run tomorrow."

Eddie frowned. "What time? You know I hate early," and picked up a jogging pace toward their coach.

For the next hour Jonathon focused on sprints and starts, trying to block out thoughts of spies and failed relationships. Not his problems, he thought.

But on his way home his mind wandered back to his thoughts of the day. What did a spy look like? Did he have a magnifying glass in his hand? Did he look like he was peering too closely at things? What would he look at? Wait! What if the spy was female? Wasn't that Japanese woman, Tokyo Rose, supposed to be a spy? And a sexy one at that! Anybody could be a spy.

He shook his head, trying to clear his mind of the confusion, but stopped short when he spotted the Studebaker was in the same spot as this morning. Well, as far he could tell it was the same spot. Had the car been there all day?

Then he saw a strange car parked in front of his house. A military car. Granny's car was there as well, but the military car really spooked him. The sight of a couple of Marine officers standing on his front stoop hurried him along.

Maybe they were just checking that Richard was telling the truth about how old he was, or that he had permission to join the service. Please God that was all it was.

Jonathon reached the front door just as Mary Anne opened it. They both said, "Good afternoon," making the marines jump. Their insignia indicated to Jonathon they were both majors.

"Is your mother home?" the taller officer asked.

"Yes sir," answered Mary Anne.

"Excuse me sir," said Jonathon. "May I ask what this is about?"

The shorter officer's shoulders drooped and he shook his head. "We'd rather talk to your mother first."

Jonathon pushed his way past and put his arm around his sister, "Please wait and we'll let our mother know you're here."

He turned to Mary Anne as he closed the front door, "Come with me, Sis," sensing she was about to bolt.

Their mother and grandmother were in the kitchen and Granny was sobbing. *Now what?* thought Jonathon.

He looked at his sister and saw Christopher standing in the doorway to the dining room looking like somebody had clobbered him. What was going on?

"Mom? There are a couple of Marine majors on the front step asking to speak to you. Is everything alright? Is Dad okay?"

"Oh honey, we've had horrible news. That's what the officers are here for I'm sure. Show them into the living room and we'll be right in."

Jonathon had to force himself to move. He felt as if his feet were frozen to the floor. When he finally got back to the front door, it took all his courage to open it and escort their guests further into the living room. "Sit down, please, sirs. My mom will be right out." He tried to appear calm, but his heart was shaking. What horrible news? *Dear Lord, please let Dad be okay.*

"We'd like to speak to her alone first, young man. She can fill you in on the details."

"No," said Mom as she walked into the room, Granny right behind her. "We know what you're going to say and we want to hear the official news together."

"Yes ma'am. But I don't know how you could have heard this. It's top secret."

The shorter major turned to Granny. "We're sorry for your loss, Mrs. Potter. Your husband was a good man. I served under him, myself. My first assignment out of Annapolis."

Grandaddy? What's happened to Granddaddy?

"But this is not about him," said the taller captain, handing Jonathon's mother his credentials. "Allow me to introduce myself, I'm Major Jedediah Bruckner and this Major Jerome O'Neal."

By now the whole family was crowded onto the sofa and Jonathon was wishing Richard and Caroline were with them. *When had Granny gotten news that Granddaddy died? Was that why she was here? What was going on?*

"We're listening, Captain Bruckner. Thank you for the condolences, but what is this about? Has something happened to my husband?"

No, thought Jonathon. *That would be too much. Not Granddaddy and Daddy. God wouldn't allow that! Would he?*

His sister was sitting in Jonathon's lap now, and Christopher was as close as he could get. Jonathon sat up ramrod straight, trying not to shake.

Major Bruckner cleared his throat and Captain O'Neal looked like he wanted to run out the door. "Yes ma'am," said Bruckner, "Major Thomas was on a secret mission and has gone missing. Two of his subordinates' bodies were found with single gunshot wounds to the head."

He held up his hand when Jonathon's mother started to stand up. "There's no evidence he's been hurt. But he's not where he was supposed to be, and he's not reported in."

Major O'Neal added, "We'd like to know if you've heard from him since your last official communication." He referred to a sheet of paper. "That was a month ago? August 22? Is that correct?"

Mary Anne nodded, "I remember seeing the letter, right Mom?"

"That's right, honey. But I did get a strange phone call two weeks ago. I could hear someone breathing and it almost sounded as if someone was whispering 'Baby Girl' into the telephone. I thought that was strange."

"Did you ask who the caller was?"

"I didn't get a chance. Whoever it was hung up after that." Mom's hand flew up to her mouth and she gasped. Then she stood up and shook the Marines' hands. "Please keep us informed and thank you for coming." She walked toward the front door, her steps firm and hurried.

As she opened it, she said. "You may have more questions to ask, but my family has had enough for today. We need to let it sink in about my father and make arrangements. I don't think we can focus on anything else." She ushered the two officers out the door and shut it firmly behind them.

"And I can't handle the thought of anything having happened to Paul. Not today, not ever." She gently put her hand on Mary Anne's cheek. "When the marines come back, and they will, please do not say a word without checking with me. The more I think about it, the more I'm certain that was your father who called. That was a secret code we'd made up in case he got into trouble. I'd forgotten all about it."

"What kind of code?" Jonathon looked in Mom's eyes to see if she would keep eye contact with him.

She did but frowned and shook her head. "We'll talk about it later, honey."

"What about Granddaddy?" asked Christopher. "How did he die?"

Granny wiped her eyes again, using her already saturated handkerchief. "There was a telegram waiting for me when I got home from my job at the Red Cross. All it said was the headquarters on Corregidor had been bombed and they had found his body curled around our dog. Colin went with him everywhere, as you know."

She patted Mary Anne's hand and continued. "His body will be sent to the Naval Academy for burial." She let out another sob, squared her shoulders and said, "I begged him to come home with me, but he wanted to finish one more piece of business before he retired."

Jonathon felt as if a heavy black mist had swallowed them up. How could they lose their grandfather and their father in such a short period of time? "What do we do now?" he asked. "What will happen to us?"

"Is Caroline safe in Guam?" Mary Anne asked.

"We have to pray that Caroline is safe." Mom turned toward Jonathon, "In answer to your questions, we'll have to arrange for your grandfather's funeral and decide whether we all can go to the service."

"Why wouldn't we all go?" Christopher asked.

Chapter 6

"I DON'T KNOW HOW WE'D all get there. It'd take three days by train and it'd be expensive. Plus, I don't know if a whole family would be allowed to take up that much room with military personnel taking higher priority," Granny said.

"Going by car would take at least a week and probably cost even more. That's if we could get enough gas for the trip. And I don't know if I would be allowed that much time off from work," Mom added. She clapped her hands and stood. "Enough of this sadness. We need to rally around for the sake of the rest of us. Let's finish getting dinner ready and I'll tell you some funny news." She pasted a smile on her face, but there was sadness in her eyes.

Jonathon wondered how his mother could compartmentalize her emotions so easily. At least is seemed as if it was easy.

They all wandered into the kitchen and were greeted by the smell of pot roast simmering on a burner. One of their maid Naomi's specialties. Of course, in this time of rationing, it was more potatoes and vegetables than meat, but it still smelled wonderful. They knew it would also taste great. Naomi was an outstanding cook.

Jonathon was friends with her son, Charles, and they played their jazz records together when he came with her on weekends. But only when nobody else was around. Naomi wouldn't let them be together when Jonathon's white friends were there. She didn't think it was proper.

Jonathon didn't care what color Charles' skin was, but Naomi knew that her son's dark-chocolate color would get him into trouble with less understanding white folk. Charles always had to address white people, including Jonathon, as sir and ma'am. Made Jonathon and his family feel weird. They didn't see the need, even if Charles' mother was their employee.

Mary Anne and Christopher carried the plates to the dining room table and Jonathon carried in the serving dish full of pot roast. Granny brought in the silverware and serving utensils, with Mom bringing in the salad she'd made.

After they were seated, Granny bowed her head and said, "Let us pray."

They all joined hands and Jonathon felt the usual calm that came when they did this. He'd tried to make this happen even when their parents weren't able to join them, but his siblings frequently made other plans or just grabbed something to munch on while they did homework.

He bowed his head when Granny started to pray. "Dear God, since you saw fit to call my beloved Bill to your side please let him watch over us as your servant. Please keep the rest of our family safe and please do not let anyone else die in the horrible war. Amen"

Mom served up the pot roast and Jonathon passed the salad around. He took the minimum amount, choosing from the outside edges to avoid the salad dressing Mom made. Much as he loved his mother's cooking, he thought salad dressings were not her long suit. Too vinegary for his taste.

After Mom picked up her knife and fork and cut up her meat, everybody else began to eat. "But now for my funny news. You remember the big deal the Lockheed made out of promoting me to being a tool and dye designer because I was their first female to hold that position?

They all nodded and smiled.

"Well, my boss called me into his office today and sat me down. Three other men and a woman from the Red Cross were there. One of the men had a camera and the woman had a notebook to write in. 'Marian', Mr.

Petersen said, 'these people are from Washington, D.C. and our own *Los Angeles Times.* You've been picked to be a "Rosie the Riveter" model.'" She grinned and blushed. "He said it didn't hurt that I was a pretty blonde."

"Wow, Mom. That's quite an honor, I guess." Christopher grinned back at her. "But what do you have to do?"

Mom frowned and her smile slipped slightly. "That's the downside. "I'll have to do war-effort promotional work. Which means more time away from home."

"I'll try to pick up the slack," Jonathon said.

"We'll help also, won't we, Christopher?" Mary Anne chimed in. Her twin nodded and grinned.

"I'm proud of you, Marian. I just wish your dad was here to share the news," added Granny, wiping another tear from her face.

The family ate in silence until Granny said, "Oh! I just had a thought. Why don't I move in with you, Marian, and help out? My lease is almost up and with your father not ever coming home, it makes sense for me to stay with you. Conserve money that way and we can pool our ration cards."

Jonathon thought he saw a slight frown on his mother's face for a split second, but then she smiled.

"It might be a tight squeeze, but we'll make do. You can sleep in the bedroom in front of my sunroom. The sunroom's my favorite place to sleep anyway."

She rose from her chair when Mary Anne and Christopher stood up to clear the table. It was their turn to do the dishes. "Wait before you two do the dishes. I bought a cake for dessert to celebrate my being 'Rosie the Riveter'." And especially after all the bad news we've had today, I'm glad I did. I think we deserve it."

Proudly toting the chocolate cake on which she had place a celebratory candle, which flickered in the air of her passage, Mom set it down in front of Granny. "Here Mother, you cut it while I bring in the plates."

"I'll get the dessert forks," Jonathon said, pulling out a drawer in the cherry credenza which was his mother's pride and joy. Jonathon loved the curve of its bowed front and the special drawers at the top designed to keep small forks and knives, and serving utensils for things like oysters or shrimp.

At six foot four and a sturdy 220 pounds, he figured people probably thought it strange that he liked delicate things like fur coats and fine china, but he didn't care. He loved the feel of fur and bone china. And it always amazed him that he could see through the bottom of the china. Besides, Granddaddy wore clear nail polish and always had a dot of Chanel #5 perfume under his nose and there wasn't a sissy thing about him. Tonight, though, Jonathon was more worried about the events of the day and what was happening to his family.

Where was Richard, for instance? Had he really enlisted? Why wasn't he home to share that news?

And what had happened to Dad? Was he alright?

And how would Granny deal with the death of Granddaddy? He'd always seemed to be her heart and soul.

Was Caroline safe? Had she heard all the family news? How could he deal with all of this and also think about spies? He wished he could at least talk to his father. The most sensible person he'd ever known. He needed some time alone, he decided. Then maybe he could shake off the feeling his latest earthquake nightmare had given him. The sensation that someone was lurking behind him.

He waited until Christopher stopped talking and then asked, "Thanks for the cake, Mom, but may I please be excused?"

His mother looked up and frowned. "Of course, dear. But is something wrong? Are you upset about something? Well, other than death of your grandfather. And that your father is missing."

"That's sure enough to give me the willies," said Christopher.

Jonathon shook his head. "Everything's fine. It's just a lot's going on and I need time to think. To sort it out."

Just as he rose, the front door banged open and Richard came racing in. He hugged Granny, tears streaming down his face. "I heard about Granddaddy at the recruiting station. I can't believe it. It can't have happened."

Granny patted his cheek. "I'm afraid it did. But he's still with us in our hearts. We'll all miss him." Her chin trembled and she stifled a sob.

"Richard," said Mom, her voice low and shivery. "What were you doing at the recruiting station? I thought we'd agreed you wouldn't enlist?"

"It doesn't matter, Mom. I didn't sign up. Not after I heard about Granddaddy. Much as I'd like to kill Japs for killing my grandfather, I figured you'd need me to get a job and help around here."

Jonathon thought he heard Mom whisper, "Thank God for that."

"How did you hear about Granddaddy, Richard?" Granny asked.

"One of the recruiters served under him and had heard the news from a buddy in the Philippines. He thought I looked like Granddaddy."

Granny wiped away another tear and nodded. "You do, Dear. You do. And Mary Anne has a lot of his traits."

"How about me, Granny?" asked Christopher. "Shouldn't I have a lot of his traits since Mary Anne and I are twins?"

Mom nodded. "You'd think so, wouldn't you? But I guess because you're fraternal, not identical twins, you do seem to favor your father's side of the family more. Just as Jonathon and Caroline do."

"Wonder why that is," muttered Jonathon.

"Scientists are just beginning to do research to see if there is something in our make-up that we carry along to our children. I believe they're calling it genetics. It's really fascinating research."

"Leave it to our chemist mother, to know this," said Richard, smiling.

It was nice to see Mom and Richard being nice to each other. Made life so much more pleasant. But Jonathon had homework to do and he wanted to call Jennifer. So, again, he asked to be excused and use the phone.

"Oh," teased Richard, "whom are you going to call, Jonathon?"

Christopher chimed in. "Wouldn't be Jennifer would it?"

"Who else?" said Mary Anne.

Mom rolled her eyes, smiled and nodded. "Don't tie up the phone too long, Jonathon. We might get news about your dad."

Chapter 8

"WAIT," SAID RICHARD, "HAS something happened to Dad?"

"He's missing," said the twins.

Richard's eyebrows shot up and his mouth gaped.

Mom held her hand up before Richard could speak. "Go ahead, Jonathon, I'll fill Richard in on the news."

Jonathon thanked his mother for a nice meal and went into the den. He pulled up the chair by Mom's beautiful cherrywood desk. A gift from Dad before he left for the Pacific.

And where was Dad now? If the Marines didn't know, who would? Was he okay? Jonathon sighed as he sat at Mom's desk. He wished the war was over. And he knew he wasn't the only one who felt this way.

Well maybe Jennifer would perk him up. She was good at that. He felt a spark of hope when the party line was open. But his shoulders sagged when Jennifer's line was busy. It was probably too late to run over to her house, even though it was still light enough. The nice thing about this year-round daylight savings time—what were they calling it? Oh, War Time—is how much longer it was light outside. Jonathon's body shrunk into itself. Guess he'd just have to wait until tomorrow when they went to the movies. His body warmed at the thought of sitting close to his beautiful girlfriend, making him miss her even more.

As he walked toward his bedroom, his thoughts drifted back to his mother's frown at Granny living with them. Why was Mom displeased with having her mother around? After all, she might take a load off Mom's shoulders.

He turned to his math book and opened it to the page of problems on working with sines. An hour later he shut the book, satisfied he'd gotten all the problems solved correctly. He felt he had his mom's gift for the sciences, but he also felt he had his dad's gift for writing. Maybe he could combine the two when he was through with school. He got up to stretch before he started on his English essay. He hadn't a clue what he was going to write his essay on. What more could he say about the war? What more could he say about his friends? Or his house or whatever else the teachers wanted him to write about.

The newly full moon was so bright, he could see Dr. Ringwaldt's house clearly out his side window. Strange not to see any lights on as daylight faded into night. Dr. Ringwaldt was usually sitting in his den by then reading and listening to the radio.

Jonathon looked down at his neighbor's driveway. The Studebaker was no longer there. Had Dr. Ringwaldt gone out? It was Friday night. Maybe after being widowed for five years he'd decided to date again. After all, he wasn't all that old. In his fifties or early sixties, maybe. But at that age would he still be interested in women? What did old people do when they dated, Jonathon wondered. Certainly, they wouldn't be interested in sex. Would they?

But Dr. Ringwaldt did have male friends who came over occasionally. Sometimes they would sit outside having cocktails on the slate patio at the back of his house. Jonathon felt a spark of happiness that his friend had male friends. It was easier to talk to men than it was to women. At least Jonathon thought he could be freer and more open when he talked to his male friends.

Girls wanted different things. They wanted to talk about settling down, making a home and raising children. They didn't want to see the world or explore different subjects.

But that wasn't true always. Look at Mom, Jonathon thought. She went to M.I.T., after all. And studied physical chemistry. She said it was strange to be only one of three women in the whole school and the other two were in graduate programs.

But even so, when Daddy came courting, she gave it all up to become a wife and mother. Jonathon wondered if she ever regretted it.

Mom never showed her emotions anymore and Jonathon didn't know how to ask her about how she was feeling. The one time he'd asked she said, "Don't let how I'm doing concern you dear, I'm fine. Let's just worry about you." The only time, lately, she'd shown her feelings was the fight she'd been having with Richard about not joining the service. And everybody was emotional about that. Now Jonathon wondered if Richard would be drafted if he weren't in school. Maybe he could prove he was needed to help support the family. Dad's salary paid for most of their costs he guessed. But it was nice to always have a little extra, just in case.

Jonathon was jerked back out of his thoughts when he saw movement at the back of Dr. Ringwaldt's house. All he could see was a darker outline in front of the silhouettes of bushes. Bushes he knew to be roses, having helped Dr. Ringwaldt prune them. The man did love to garden and his greenhouse orchids were world renowned.

There still were no lights on either inside or outside the house, but here was this figure creeping around. Had to be a man judging from the size. What should Jonathon do? He decided to get Richard and see what was going on.

Chapter 9

RICHARD WASN'T IN HIS room. Maybe he was downstairs listening to the radio or reading. Nope, he wasn't in the living room or the sun room either. The door to the den was closed, but Mom was probably in there working on something.

Jonathon knocked softly on the door and then peeked in. Mom wasn't in there and then he remembered he she had night shift tonight. He wondered if her co-workers would treat her differently now that she was a Rosie the Riveter?

And would she have to do other things than pose for pictures? Probably. She'd most likely have to do more war bond promotional work. When would she find the time? He wondered if she'd get more money for this? Not likely. And just think it was part of being a "Good American."

Jonathon shook his head. *Focus*, he told himself, *you're looking for Richard.*

But his brother wasn't in the room either. Was it he wandering around Dr. Ringwaldt's back yard? Why would he do that? Why wouldn't he just ring the doorbell?

Jonathon slipped out the front door and silently moved toward his neighbor's house. He looked in the back yard first, but couldn't see anybody there. At least not in the patio area. He slipped back into the small tangerine orchard and thought he saw a moving shadow near one of the trees. Still no lights showing anywhere on the property. But when he got closer to the tree, he realized it was only some branches swaying in a light breeze.

He heard something click further back in the yard. Probably just another branch he thought and was about to turn back toward the house when he heard a crunching sound. Like shoe leather on asphalt. Had someone gone out the back gate?

He was about to head out that way when he heard someone behind him hiss, "Jonathon? Is that you?"

Sounded like Richard.

Jonathon turned toward his brother and saw his silhouette up near Dr. Ringwaldt's patio. "What are you doing?" he whispered when he got closer.

Richard came up next to Jonathon, "I saw somebody out here from the upstairs window and came to investigate. And you?"

"Me too. Plus, there haven't been any lights on all night and I haven't seen Dr. Ringwaldt in a couple of days."

"Maybe we should check his garage," said Richard, "and see if his car is gone."

"Good idea." Jonathon headed to the side of the house where the garage was. "Did you see the Studebaker here earlier today?"

"It was pulling into the driveway when I left this morning, but I didn't see who was driving."

"It was just sitting there when we headed to school today and but it was gone when I got home around 4:30."

The brothers peered through the garage window to see their neighbor's car parked as it usually was, with its nose pointing toward the street.

"Maybe Dr. Ringwaldt went some place with whoever was driving that Studebaker?" asked Jonathon.

"Could be," said Richard. "Let's figure out if we can see inside his house."

The brothers walked to the front of the house and peered in through the floor to ceiling windows that looked into the living room near the fireplace. The moon was so bright it acted as spotlight into the room.

"Hmm," said Jonathon. "Does that look like a foot showing just left of the chair? Dr. Ringwaldt's favorite chair, isn't it?"

Richard cupped his hands around his eyes to get a clearer look. "I can't tell. Maybe he fell asleep in his chair. Let's just leave him for tonight."

"We can knock on his door tomorrow morning and see if he's alright. No sense waking him up now," responded Jonathon.

Richard stretched as he stood up. "I don't know about you, but I'm ready to hit the hay. Let's go home."

"Good idea."

They were headed back to their house when Jonathon turned and realized he had to look down slightly to see his brother's face. When had he gotten taller than Richard? He guessed it had been a while since they were this close together.

"What are you going to do now, Richard? If you're not going to enlist, are you going back to school."

Richard shook his head. "No. I've been offered an important job and I start on Monday."

"Great! What's the job?"

Richard shook his head and reached for their front door handle. "All I can tell you is my studies will come in handy."

Jonathon's mouth gaped open. "Why can't you tell me more?"

"It's a government job and I'm not allowed to talk about it."

Chapter 10

JONATHON EYED HIS BROTHER with suspicion and shook his head. "You're pulling my leg. What is the job?"

Richard shook his head. "Sorry, no can do. And I am telling the truth."

They headed upstairs to their separate rooms. That was when Jonathon remembered he hadn't finished his essay for English, but all of a sudden, he knew what he was writing about. Suspicious behavior. Like strange cars in his neighbor's driveway and his brother not telling him what was going on and Dad maybe leaving furtive messages for Mom. He was done in half an hour and dropped into bed exhausted. Tomorrow would be better. He could sleep in a little while. Then he had a date with Jennifer. Maybe Eddie and Sammy would have made up by then and could go to the movies with them. They were going to see Humphrey Bogart and this new actress, Lauren Bacall, in "To Have and Have Not."

His last thought before he fell asleep was, "Everything will be alright." But dark dreams clouded his mind and he jerked around in his sleep. His recurring dream of being alone in a desert and having the earth rumble and split open all around him haunted his sleep. He kept trying to get away, but each time he turned in a different direction the earth would split open again. Soon he was on the last bit of land available and the earthquake rumbling had started again. He knew he was doomed. He bolted upright in his bed; his heart ready to explode. His eyes were so wide open he was sure they'd pop out of his head.

The nightmare had started two years ago after they had moved back to L.A. from the east coast. They'd just settled into this house when an earthquake had hit close in front of their house. When the family went out of the house after it was over, Jonathon was the first to see the side-walk buckled up right in front of a massive oak tree.

When he pointed it out, his dad remarked that it was a good thing the tree hadn't fallen, it would have crushed the front of their house. Jonathon had never been afraid of things before, but that earthquake had really scared him. He'd never felt very brave again. And the fear felt cemented into his soul when the tree came down last spring. The top missed crushing the house by an inch. He should have been relieved because only the tip brushed up against the front door, but instead it took him at least half an hour to get his heart rate back to normal.

He could tackle other guys in football and he felt he could defend himself or his family from anybody wanting to harm them. But things like earthquakes or hurricanes or even thunderstorms made him uneasy. Scared even, if he was being truthful. He couldn't protect anybody from the forces of nature. It made him feel small that he was so not in control.

He checked his alarm clock and realized it was already nine a.m. Time to get moving, even if he still felt sleepy. Probably because of not sleeping well. He grabbed his jeans, a tee-shirt and a clean pair of white socks, and headed to the bathroom he shared with his siblings. But, of course, when he tried to open the bathroom door it was locked. He could hear Mary Anne splashing in the tub, singing a Bing Crosby song. "I'm dreaming of a white Christmas," she warbled.

Geeze, thought Jonathon. She doesn't even have the right season much less the correct key. Mary Anne was talented in a lot of ways, but singing sure wasn't one of them. He knocked on the door, but she didn't respond.

He knocked louder.

Still no response.

He clenched his fist and pounded so hard he could see the door panel flex inward against his strength. "Come on, Mary Anne! Your time is up! I gotta pee."

"Alright, Jonathon, alright. I'll be out in a few minutes." He heard a splash and the plug slurp out of the drain. Then the water started its gurgle down the drain and something, probably Mary Anne's wet foot, splatted on the tile floor.

A minute later and Jonathon was trying to think of anything but water gurgling. "I'm about the wet the floor here, Mary Anne. Grab your stuff and finish dressing in your room."

"Aye, aye Captain," said his sister as she creaked open the door. "Your wish is my command."

"Oh sure," said Jonathon. "You always let me have my way. I just haven't noticed." He stepped aside as Mary Anne brushed past him. Her wet hair dribbling on his feet.

He slammed the door, almost catching Mary Anne's bathrobe hem in the door jam. He wanted to get in and out of the bathtub and the bathroom as quickly as he could. His mind already thinking of Jennifer. He wanted to get a rose just to show he was thinking of her.

He was ready in less than half an hour, including freshly shined penny loafers with a shiny new penny in the slots on the top of the shoes. He peered over the bannister at the top of the staircase to see if Mom was around. Nope, he didn't hear her, so he turned backward, flipped his left leg over the bannister and slid down. Loved doing that.

He headed down the hallway toward the kitchen and glanced into the sunroom. Through the far windows he could see Dr. Ringwaldt's driveway which reminded him of what he had seen last night. He wondered if Richard had already checked to see if their neighbor was okay. He wolfed down a handful of strawberries and a glass of orange juice, grabbed a muffin and rushed out the front door, leaving behind a trail of crumbs.

When he reached Dr. Ringwaldt's front door, he noticed it was slightly ajar. Hadn't been like that last night, had it? He stopped for a minute to think back. No, he was sure it was closed. Or did Richard say he'd checked. Jonathon couldn't remember.

He knocked and called loudly, "Dr. Ringwaldt? It's your neighbor, Jonathon Thomas. Are you alright?"

The door jerked open, making Jonathon stumble.

Richard was holding the knob. He pulled his brother inside, hissing out "shssh!" Then he quietly shut the door.

Jonathon whispered, "What are you doing, Richard? Where's Dr. Ringwaldt?"

"In his chair. That was his foot we saw last night."

"What!" yelled Jonathon, "Is..." Richard clamped his hand over his brother's mouth, before he could say anything else.

"He's dead. Knife wound to the heart."

Jonathon's eyes widened to the largest point possible. "Who would hurt him? He was always nice," he whispered. "And why are we whispering if we won't disturb him?

Richard shrugged, "I don't know who killed him and I think the killer may still be around."

"Why do you think that?"

"I heard the back door shut when I first got here. I didn't think anything of it until I saw Dr. Ringwaldt." Richard pulled Jonathon toward their neighbor's body.

"Wait, Richard. Shouldn't we call the police? Shouldn't we wait until they get here?"

"I have called them, but they didn't sound eager to come. Said they'd be here when they could."

"That's weird."

The brothers turned toward the front windows when they heard a car pull into the driveway. But it wasn't a patrol car. It was the grey Studebaker.

"What's it doing here? Jonathon asked nobody in particular.

Richard shrugged, but they both moved out of the line of sight for anybody looking in.

A short, squat man with a heavy red beard and thick red hair waddled toward the front door, but stopped when he saw the open front door. He looked around the yard as if expecting to see Dr. Ringwaldt tending to his garden. He stood on the pathway looking back at his car and forward toward the house, as if he didn't know whether to stay or leave. His torso twisted back towards his car and his left foot moved in that direction, but froze when a squad car pulled in behind his car. He looked as if he'd been turned into the proverbial "Pillar of Salt."

The brothers saw stark fear spread across the man's face and he raised his arms in surrender. They looked at each. "Do you think he murdered Dr. Ringwaldt?" Jonathon asked.

Richard shook his head and for a third time since they'd been there, shrugged his shoulders. "Let's go introduce ourselves to the officers."

They met the policemen at the front after the redhead had been stuffed into the back of the squad car.

"Hello officers," said Richard. "I'm Richard Thomas and this is my brother Jonathon."

"Hey, I know you, Richard. I was in your calculus class last semester."

Richard looked closer at the policeman. "Oh Jack! I didn't recognize you with your uniform on. How's it going?"

"Fine," said Jack. "Doing what I always wanted to do. But now I'm going to college at night. Might become a lawyer."

"Come on, Jack. You know everybody and we've got work to do, even if that guy gave himself up." The other policeman reached out his hand to shake Richard's. "What's happened here?"

Richard explained how they happened to be there and what they'd seen the night before. "But," and paused to look at the officer's nametag, "Officer O'Reilly, Jonathon and I thought we heard someone leave by the back gate, when we came over. The Studebaker wasn't in the driveway then."

"So, you don't think Reds is the killer?" asked Jack.

"I have no idea," said Jonathon, with a shake of his head. "But why else would he surrender?"

"Maybe he stole the car?" asked Jack.

"Do you want us to show you where Dr. Ringwaldt is?" asked Richard and lead the way to the body after both policemen nodded.

Jonathon couldn't think of it as Dr. Ringwaldt's body. In his mind it was just "the body." He hated to think of the kind man being murdered. He'd been so nice to everybody. Always ready to lend a hand, and Jonathon had seen him give change to the drunks on Wilshire Boulevard more than once. Why would anybody want to murder him?

Wasn't sure he wanted to see the body, but didn't want to seem like a baby, so he trudged along behind the others. Fortunately, as they were just about to turn in front of Dr. Ringwaldt, Jonathon spied Mary Anne headed toward the front door.

Officer O'Reilly saw her at the same time and snapped. "What is this? A parade? Keep her away," he said, looking at Officer Jack.

"That's our sister," said Richard. "We'll keep her away."

"I'll stop her," Jonathon said, trying not to sound too eager. He hurried out the front door and stopped his sister before she got to the front path. "Hey Sis, what do you need?"

"Nothing. I was just curious to see what was going on."

"Dr. Ringwaldt died and the police are investigating."

"Why?"

"Why, what?" asked her brother.

"Why do the police care?"

"Because of the way he died." Jonathon gently encircled his sister's slim arm with his hand and turned her back toward their house. "I could use a snack. I didn't have much breakfast. Come sit with me. Seems we never talk much anymore."

Mary Anne smiled and said "Very tactful, Jonathon. I get the hint." She stretched her stride to keep up. She loved to do things with her brothers, especially Jonathon.

When they got to the kitchen, they scrambled some eggs and toasted some bread. They were out of their month's ration of jam, so Mary Anne broke a dye packet into the solidified grease that made up Oleo. She hated the stuff, but found it soothing to mix the dye in. Calmed her down some.

"What do you have up for the rest of the day, Mary Anne?"

"I told Ginger I'd meet her at the soda shop at noon." She looked at the kitchen clock. "Oh, I'd better hurry, it's almost 10:30 now." She grabbed her plate, stacked it on top of Jonathon's and headed to the sink. Her brother followed with the juice glasses.

"Yeah, I told Jennifer I'd come by for her at noon. I'll do the dishes and you go on. I think it's my turn anyway."

Mary Anne gave her brother a brief hug and hurried to her room. She came back a few minutes later, purse in hand and pale lipstick on her lips. Mom wouldn't allow anything other than pale on the fifteen-year-old. "Too brazen," she said, which of course made the girl roll her eyes. But Mary Anne had stopped saying, "But all the other mothers think it's okay." Thanks to Caroline's help she was allowed at least some make-up.

Jonathon smiled at her and said, "You look very pretty, Sis. Have fun."

"Thanks. Oh, I almost forgot! Mom called to say we're to meet her down at the shipyard at 5 p.m. and wear our Sunday clothes."

"Why? And do we have to?"

"She's christening one of those new ships. What's it called, oh an aircraft carrier, and, yes, we do. Richard has to go as well, if he's here."

"Shoot," muttered Jonathon, "didn't think Mom's Rosie the Riveter duties would involve us."

How're we going to get there? Wonder if Mom'll pay for a taxi. Jonathon wiped the last dish and put it away. It was a good thing he'd bathed this morning. He headed upstairs to change his clothes wondering whether his white dress shirt still fit, or if the weight lifting he'd been doing had made his chest too thick.

Tight, but he'd manage. He squeezed into his dress shoes and prayed he'd not develop a blister as he had earlier in the year, when they'd gone to the ballet. How his mother had gotten those tickets he had no idea. But she was bound and determined to make sure her children were exposed to the fine arts. Actually, they all enjoyed what they'd seen. Jonathon even liked to listen to the Metropolitan Opera broadcasts on Saturday afternoon. Though he did have to admit that some of the women sounded like sick cats.

As he came back down the stairs, Richard and Christopher came in the front door together. "Wow, Jonathon!" said Christopher, as Richard gave a wolf whistle. "You and Jennifer decide to tie the knot today?"

Jonathon shook his head. "Sorry you two, but you're going to have gussy up as well. Rosie the Riveter duty calls us all. Mom wants us to meet her down at the shipyard by 5. She's christening the new air craft carrier that's set to launch today. And she wants the whole family there."

"But I have plans," whined Christopher.

"Just reporting what I'm told to, sir."

"How are we supposed to get there?" asked Richard.

Jonathon shrugged. "Dunno. Maybe we can scrounge enough money together to afford a taxi. I was going to take Jennifer to the movies today and buy her a rose, but I won't be able to do that now." He pulled money out of his pocket and counted. "Four dollars total. If I buy Jennifer an ice cream as a sorry present, that'll leave three dollars and eighty cents.

He looked at his brothers, "How much you got?" Richard had five dollars and Christopher had two. "Wow, we're rich! If Mary Anne has any left, we'll be able to go out to dinner at the diner."

"Let's meet at the corner of Wilshire and Wilton Place at 3:30," Christopher suggested. "That'll give us time to get to the port, so Mom won't worry whether we're going to show."

Jonathon nodded. "See you then. And remember to use the spit and polish. We want to make Mom proud."

Christopher climbed the steps two at time and headed to his room. Two minutes later he was running water for his bath.

Richard started toward the kitchen, but Jonathon grabbed his arm. "Tell me what happened after I left, Richard."

"They examined the crime scene and the coroner came. He carefully pulled the knife out of Dr. Ringwaldt's chest and wrapped it up so they could examine it for fingerprints. At least that's what Jack told me they were going to do. Then they looked around for evidence, but everything looked normal to me."

"What did they do with the body?"

"Wrapped it up, put in on a stretcher and took it away in an ambulance." Richard shuddered and wiped his right hand over his face. "I hope to never see something like that again."

"What did they do with Reds? Did they let him go?"

Richard shook his head, "No. They took him away in the patrol car. And they have a guard on the door."

"Why? Nobody else lives there."

Richard wrinkled up the corner of his mouth. "No idea, and Jack wasn't telling me anything else. He got in trouble with the other officer after telling me procedural stuff."

"The whole thing seems peculiar to me," said Jonathon. "Hope the redhead makes out alright. Somehow, I don't think he's the murderer." He patted his brother shoulder and sighed. "Well I'd better go tell Jennifer the news about no movie and no date. Hope she understands."

Chapter 11

JONATHON HEADED OUT THE front door and Richard went upstairs
to change. Christopher warbling just as poorly as his twin was the last
thing Jonathon heard as he closed the door.

Five minutes later, pink rose in hand, Jonathon was explaining to
Jennifer why he had to cancel their date. He handed her the rose and
said, "But we do have time for an ice cream."

"That'd be fine, Jonathon, and you can tell me why you look so
troubled."

"Troubled? Do I look troubled?" Jonathon was surprised his feelings
showed so easily on his face.

Jennifer nodded.

Mary Anne was still with her friends in the soda shop, so Jonathon
stopped by her table. He greeted her friends and told her where they
would meet Christopher and Richard at 3:30.

Her friend, Mildred, said, "Why don't you sit with us, Jonathon? We
hardly ever get to see you."

Jonathon laughed and said, "Thanks, but Jennifer and I have stuff to
talk about."

Mildred's smile sag and she said, "Oh, I didn't see Jennifer was with you. She can sit with us, also."

Mary Anne frowned at her friend. "Give it up, Mildred," she said.

When they were seated at a smaller table as far away as they could get from Mary Anne's table, Jennifer urged Jonathon again. "Now, my friend, what's troubling you? That is other than having girls hang all over you."

Jonathon smiled with one side of his mouth before saying, "You're the girl for me, Jennifer. And I didn't want to bother you with what's going on."

She laid her hand on his shoulder. "What kind of girlfriend would I be, if you couldn't bother me with stuff?"

"You're the best girlfriend I could ever want." He smiled, squeezed her hand, and said, "Thanks for being you, sweetheart." Then he told her about what had happened from the time he left his house with the twins Friday morning. He mentioned how strange it'd seemed to see the Studebaker in the driveway. So out of place for their neighbor.

"Do you think the guy with the Studebaker killed Dr. Ringwaldt?"

"No." Jonathon shook his head several times.

"Why?"

"Well, why would he come back? Why wouldn't he stay away?"

"Maybe he wasn't sure Dr. Ringwaldt was dead. Maybe he thought he'd just wounded him and he wanted to finish the job."

"Why would he leave in his car and come back on foot last night? And then come back again in his car this morning?"

"You're right. But then again, why would anybody want to murder a nice old man like Dr. Ringwaldt?"

Jonathon shrugged his shoulders for what seemed like the zillionth time that day. "None of this makes sense." He looked at his watch. "I'd better go. I've got to meet the others at 3:30." He laid fifty-five cents on the table to cover the ice cream and five-cent tip.

Jennifer stood up as well. "I'll walk along with you part way. Give us some more time together."

Jonathon smiled and kissed her cheek as she walked along with him. "Thanks for listening. I do feel better."

Jennifer smiled as well and squeezed his hand.

When they got to where Jennifer had to turn off, they still had twenty minutes. Jonathon wiped off a park bench set next to a palm tree so Jennifer wouldn't get dirty. He admired how neat she always was and how pretty she looked in her black slacks and ruffled blouse. Its light blue color highlighted her grey eyes. Everybody said her eyes were the same shade as Elizabeth Taylor's, but Jonathon thought Jennifer's eyes were prettier.

Jonathon slipped his arm around his girl's shoulders and pulled her close. She sighed and leaned her head against his arm, the hair on the top of her head tickling his chin. He loved the color of her hair. Almost like the color of a chestnut—a rich chocolate brown with red highlights. He felt so lucky to have met her.

But what would happen after high school? Would she go off to college in a different state? Would he? Would she want to get married right after high school? He wouldn't. He wanted to see the world.

Jennifer stirred and looked up at him. "Time for you to go, Jonathon. And I'm going to the library to look at college brochures. My dad finally said it wasn't a waste time for a girl to get more education. He and Mom have already seen too many women widowed during this war. Plus, more women needed jobs during the depression."

"Not to mention that girls are just as smart as guys," added Jonathon.

She kissed him on the end of his nose and then stood up. "Let me know what you learn about your neighbor's murder and be sure to lock your doors before you go to bed."

"That's probably a good idea, Jennifer. If we can find the key." He stood beside her and pulled her in for one last hug. "Let me know what colleges look good to you."

Jennifer crossed the main street and headed down a smaller road toward her house.

Jonathon moved off in the direction they'd been going, hoping he didn't get too much street dust on his clothes. He pulled at his collar and felt moisture around his neck. It was pretty warm.

He was close enough to the area of his town where the big movie lots had their sound stages and offices. As he went by MGM, he saw three actors dressed up in cowboy clothes, including boots with spurs strapped on and chaps covering their trousers. They wore plain shirts with yokes and brown Stetsons. What most people thought cowboys dressed liked. Jonathon wondered if that was truly cowboy gear. And then he thought he saw Walter Brennan sauntering along, but he wasn't sure.

As he walked further down the street, he did see two of Granny's favorite actors. Lucille Ball and Desi Arnez walking down the street, holding hands and smiling at everybody they saw. He remembered Granny saying they were the nicest actors when it came to visiting wounded service men and women. She said they often called her to ask when they could visit the veterans' hospitals. Other actors were willing to visit if asked, but hardly anybody else volunteered to visit.

He liked to hear Granny's stories about the movie crowd. He remembered laughing when she told him about the Marx brothers when they were invited to play Bridge in people's houses. They always played pranks just as they did in their movies. Granny was not impressed nor was the hostess pleased when Harpo flipped over the card table right in the middle of a hand. People were not inviting the Marx's to parties anymore. Hard on the furniture, Granny said. And their behavior was too boorish. Probably was, he admitted, but still funny.

He got to the taxi stand just as Richard and Christopher showed up. Mary Anne was already there. A taxi cab arrived about a minute later and they all climbed in. Jonathon was allowed to ride up front. "You take up all the room, Jonathon," said Richard.

"And it's hard enough to sit between these two behemoths," said Mary Anne, as she rolled her shoulders and arms inwards and propped her feet on top of the driveshaft bump.

"Where to?" asked the driver.

"The Navy shipyard, please," Christopher said.

"Do you know which bay?"

"No sir, but they're christening a ship today, so let's just go to the busiest one."

"Hey," said Mary Anne. "Have you heard any more about what happened at Dr. Ringwaldt's house?"

"No," chorused the three brothers.

"Maybe there will be something in the paper tomorrow," Christopher added. "There were lots of reporters and photographers hanging around outside. And I even saw a newsreel crew there filming. They were trampling flowers all around his yard."

"Poor Dr. Ringwaldt," said Jonathon. "He did love his gardens."

"I'm sure he'd hate to see the mess they've made." Mary Anne shook her head and looked down at her fingers. "I still don't see why anybody would want to kill him. Are they sure it was a murder and not a suicide?"

"I definitely do not think it was a suicide," answered Richard.

Chapter 12

"LET'S NOT TALK IT about right now. Let's be happy for Mom's time in the sun," said Jonathon.

"Wonder if Granny will be there?" Christopher mused.

The cab pulled up at the main gate to the shipyard and was stopped by a Marine. "State your business, please."

"My passengers are going to the ship christening," said the cabbie.

The Marine looked into the car and peered at each passenger. "Your names, please."

"We're Marian Thomas' children. She's christening the ship today," said Mary Anne, grinning from ear to ear.

"Oh, yes," said the Marine. "We'll escort you from here."

"How much do we owe you?" Jonathon asked the cabbie.

He shook his head. "No charge. I didn't realize who you were. It's my privilege to drive Mrs. Thomas' children anywhere they want to go."

"Thank you, sir, but at least let us pay for your gas," said Richard, and handed him a dollar.

"Your mother has raised you well, as I knew she would," said the cabbie. He smiled. "I drive her home sometimes when she works the night shift. She's a good person."

After the family left the cab, another Marine escorted them to Bay 9, where a huge crowd of military personnel, newsmen and civilians milled around. Jonathon wasn't sure if they'd ever find their mother in this crowd, but several Marines cleared a path for them until they were standing beside Granny, who was looking like she would burst a seam from pride. She had a wide brimmed hat perched on her silver curls, with a broad, bright red satin band encircling the crown. The red was the same shade as the piping on her blue suit.

"Wow Granny, you're the cat's meow," said Richard and he winked at her.

Granny blushed and hugged her grandson. "You are your grandfather's kin, that's for sure, Richard Potter Thomas."

"Where's Mom?" asked Jonathon.

Granny nodded toward the bow of a huge grey ship that loomed large above them. "See where the Admiral is standing on that raised platform? Look to his right."

"Oh, I see her," exclaimed Mary Anne. "Wow she sure looks pretty in that green dress."

"Yeah, but she also looks tiny compared to the Admiral and that ship," said Christopher.

"I wonder where she got the dress?" Mary Anne said.

"Who cares?" said Christopher.

"What kind of ship is it?" asked Jonathon, looking toward the side of the ship where the deck spread out over the sides of the hull.

"I believe it's what they call an aircraft carrier. So they can launch planes from the ocean," said Richard.

"Is that even possible?" asked Mary Anne. "What would the planes do then?"

"Fly to land, silly," said Christopher, "and bomb the enemy."

"How far can the planes fly before they need to refuel?" asked Jonathon.

Everybody shrugged, but before anyone could answer, the Admiral addressed the crowd and started droning on about how exciting it was to launch a new ship and what an honor it was to have a Rosie the Riveter there to christen it.

Why couldn't he just hand the bottle of champagne to Mom and let her smash it? thought Jonathon. People could be so long winded when they were in the spotlight. He vowed never to talk on and on if he was ever in that position.

Finally, the admiral handed the bottle over and the long shiny ribbon fastened to the bow of the ship stretched taut. Mom reached back with her arm and hurled the bottle forward. "Clunk," went the bottle when it hit the hull and then it bounced backward undamaged.

Mom grabbed it again and hurled the bottle forward even harder. Another clunk and another failed attempt. People in the audience began to chuckle, which made Mom turn red along her neck and face. Again, she grabbed the bottle and pulled it back, but this time she stepped back two or three steps, frowning in concertation. She twisted her torso away from the ship and then stepped forward as if she were pitching a strike at a batter, letting her back leg step forward and her right arm release toward the bow.

KAPOW! Champagne flew everywhere, as did tiny shards of glass. The crowd roared out a cheer and backed up quickly trying to dodge the mess.

Mom grinned from ear-to-ear and posed for her picture. She beckoned for her children and mother to join her and introduced them to the admiral.

Granny smiled and said, "Admiral Bullitz and I are well acquainted, aren't we Bully?"

"Oh, of course," said Mom. "You went to Annapolis with my father, didn't you? I'd forgotten that."

"So had I," said the admiral. "But when I saw Leila, I remembered." His eyes lost their smile and he said, "I was sorry to hear about his death, Leila. I didn't know you were in town, or I would have looked you up, my dear."

A photographer approached the group and said, "Excuse me, but could I have you all stand by the ship and let me take your picture?"

They stood in front of the huge ship, which made Jonathon feel tiny. An odd feeling for him. He was used to being the tallest thing around, except for buildings of course. He didn't like that ship lurking over him like that. Like having a teacher look over his shoulder at school. Or the shadowy figure who kept showing up in his nightmare.

When they were done, Mom said, "Let's go to the Brown Derby for dinner. It's a celebration. And you all look so handsome it in your Sunday clothes."

"Can we afford it?" asked Jonathon.

"Of course, dear," said Mom. "We certainly don't waste money."

"And it's not an everyday thing to christen a ship," said Granny.

"Even if it did take you three tries," whispered Christopher to Mary Anne.

Mom looked at him and lowered her lids to half-mast.

"Just kidding," he said, looking down at the ground.

The woman who had organized the whole shebang arranged for transport to the restaurant, so the family arrived in style. There were even reporters and newsreel crews there to film the family entering the restaurant. Or maybe they were there to look for famous people. All that was missing was the searchlights that were usually in place for movie stars.

Fine with Jonathon. He wasn't really keen on being in the spotlight and Richard looked like he was trying to hide in the small knot of people waiting to get into the Brown Derby.

They were seated in one of the end banquettes, which Mary Anne loved. She didn't like being squished between her brothers. The sofa part curved in a soft arc, leaving them room to spread out but still be together. Jonathon and Richard sat on the outside of the table to give everyone enough room.

When the waiter came up and filled their water glasses, Mom and Granny order martinis and Richard ordered a beer. The rest ordered iced tea. Mary Anne's head started to swivel back and forth. She was looking for movie stars. She knew good looking Montgomery Cliff was frequently seen here, but he always sat toward the back of the room and he was usually alone.

"Look, Sis," whispered Christopher, nodding to his left, "there are Clark Gable and Carol Lombard."

"Ooh," said Mary Anne, "the newly-weds! Look how happy they are."

Mom tapped her daughter's arm. "Don't stare. It's rude."

The waiter came back with their drinks and everybody ordered. Steaks for the boys and fish for the girls.

When they were alone again, Mary Anne asked, "Mom, did you hear what happened at Dr. Ringwaldt's house? He was murdered! The police and the news crews were there."

"What!" exclaimed Mom and Granny together.

"When did this happen?" asked Mom. "His house was quiet when I left for work last night. Though there was a strange car creeping down the street."

"What kind of car?" asked Jonathon. Before Mom could reply, the waiter came back with their salads and rolls. And a small plate of real butter! A luxury, for sure.

Mom took a bite of her romaine and tomato salad. "Mmm, that's good.

"What did you ask me, Jonathon? Oh yes, what kind of car. That funny looking one. You know the one where you can't tell if it's coming or going. It was grey."

"Could you tell who was driving it?" asked Richard.

"Somebody very short. At first, I thought the car was driving itself, but then I saw the top of a man's hat. A Fedora, I think."

Jonathon and Richard nodded to each other. "Same guy," said Jonathon.

"Probably," said Richard.

Granny looked at her grandsons and raised her eyebrows. "What do you know about this?"

Richard started and Jonathon added his part of what had happened.

"We saw that car, a Studebaker isn't it, on our way to school yesterday, didn't we?" Christopher said, his voice squeaking in excitement.

Mary Anne nodded. "I remember pointing out you couldn't see which way was front."

"Why would anyone want to murder Bruno. He wouldn't harm a flea. He did so much for the wounded soldiers and sailors." Granny wiped a tear off her check, searched in her purse for her handkerchief and then dabbed at her nose.

"And why would the Studebaker man just give himself up like that? Do you think he murdered our neighbor?" asked Mom. She shivered. "I thought our street was so safe. That's why I picked the neighborhood."

Chapter 13

J ONATHON OPENED HIS MOUTH to say something, but the waiter arrived at the table carrying a folding rack, followed by two other waiters carrying plates of steaming hot food. The family sniffed in the enticing aromas of steamed fresh vegetables and spiced entres and sat back in their seats to give the servers room to put the food down.

Richard licked his lips and said, "My mouth's watering. I didn't realize I was so hungry."

Christopher raised his glass of iced tea. "I'd like to propose a toast to our mom, Rosie the Riveter!"

They all raised their glasses and sipped as Mom sat flushing beet-red and nodding her head. When they had all set their glasses down, Granny signaled that everyone could eat by cutting into her fish, exposing the deep-orangey red flesh of perfectly cooked salmon.

Silence settled in over the group while they all savored the first few bites of their dinners. The only noises were the murmurs of conversation from neighboring tables and the tinkle of silverware as other customers continued to eat.

When half his steak was gone, Richard cleared his throat and tapped his water glass with his bread knife. "I have an announcement to make."

"You've decided to marry Marlena Dietrich, after all?" joked Mary Anne.

"Ha! Ha, Twerp," answered Richard. "That's next year, after I make enough money at my new job!"

"Tell us more about the job, Richard." gasped Mom. "Is it here in L.A.?"

"When do you start?" asked Granny

"What are you doing?" asked Christopher.

"Is it with Lockheed, like Mom?" asked Mary Anne.

"In order of questions asked. It starts here while I learn the ropes. I start on Monday. I can't tell you anything other than I'm working for the government. And lastly, no it's not with Lockheed."

The family sat stunned, eating utensils hanging above their plates. Mom broke the silence. "That's wonderful news, Son. So, you will be staying with us. Is that correct?"

"I don't know where I'll be living down the road, but for the moment I'll still be at home." Richard looked at his mother. "If that's okay with you."

"Of course, Dear. But if you have to move, I'll understand."

"If you have to move, Richard, make it someplace interesting. Then we can come visit." Mary Anne said, with a wink and a smile.

"Some place safe," said Granny.

"To celebrate Richard's good news I think we should have dessert." said Mom. "I'm going to have a piece of apple pie a al mode."

"Make that two," said Christopher.

"I'll have a dish of peppermint ice cream, please," added Mary Anne.

"Chocolate ice cream for me, please," said Granny.

"I'd like an éclair, please," Jonathon added.

"Me too, please," said Richard. "Probably won't have another one of those for a long time."

After dinner was over, when the check was presented to Mom, her children all excused themselves to use the bathroom. But not before she started her standard joke. She looked at the total, put her hand to her heart and took a breath. They were far enough away from the table, they felt no-one could connect them with her enormous gasp for air or the "Good Lord!" she squeaked out.

They shook their heads in amazement that she still pulled that stunt.

And all the men in the room chuckled, knowing exactly how she felt.

The doorman hailed a cab for Granny, but the rest of the family decided to walk home. It was a pleasant evening and they rationalized walking off some of the food they'd eaten would be a good thing.

Richard slipped his arm around his mother and thanked her for a nice meal. "I'm proud to be your son, Rosie."

Jonathon laughed and said. "Yeah Mom, you've got a riveting personality."

The twins laughed along with the rest of the family. But they all quieted down when they reached Dr. Ringwaldt's house. It was dark and quiet, but it seemed spooky somehow.

"Look," whispered Mary Anne, "Somebody is standing out front near the steps. Who would that be?"

"Hello," came a deep voice. "I'm looking for my uncle. Bruno Ringwaldt? Do you know where he is this evening?"

"I'm sorry to...," started Mary Anne.

But Jonathon squeezed her arm. "Ow, Jonathon, what are you doing?"

Jonathon pulled her back. "Dr. Ringwaldt was an only child," he whispered.

But the stranger heard him. "Oh, I'm sorry. It just I've known him all my life and my parents taught me to call him "Uncle Bruno. I'm Walter Jones from Winchester, Virginia."

"Nice to meet you," said Mom, and these are my children." But when she turned to introduce them, Jonathon and Richard were pulling the twins back. "Well, anyway. Perhaps we'll see you later." She hurried to catch up with her family.

When they were all safely in their house, Christopher found the key and locked the door. Mom shook her finger at them and scowled. "I've never been so ashamed. What do you mean by being so rude to that man?"

"He's lying, Mom," Jonathon replied. "Dr. Ringwaldt had never been out of California. He was raised in Folsom and moved here to attend UCLA in 1902. He's been here ever since."

"How do you know that?" asked Mom.

"We used to have long talks on his patio," replied Jonathon. "He was a geologist and studied the earthquake patterns in this part of California. And he was a huge baseball fan. We traded baseball cards."

"Well, if that man isn't who he says he is, should we call the police?" asked Mom.

"That might be a good idea," said Richard. "I'll call and talk to Detective Abramson. He's the lead detective over Jack and his partner."

"In case we're wrong, why not just call Jack? He'll know whether our suspicions are justified," said Jonathon.

"Good thinking." Richard went to the phone, looked up the police district number and clicked the phone for the operator, but then he heard Mrs. Huntsville's voice. One of their party line partners was using the phone line. Richard groaned. She could talk for hours and she didn't care if other people needed to use the phone.

"Excuse me, Mrs. Huntsville, this is your neighbor, Richard Thomas. I hate to do this, but I have an important call to make. Could you please let me use to phone? I promise not to take up too much time and I promise to let you have the line for the rest of the night."

"Well, really!" protested Mrs. Huntsville. "I hardly ever use the phone."

Richard rolled his eyes and sank into the chair by the phone desk.

"As I said, Mrs. Huntsville, this really is an important call and the problem just arose."

"What problem is that?" Mrs. Huntsville asked.

"It's personal in nature. I really would appreciate your cooperation, ma'am."

"Hmph," she responded and hung up the phone.

Richard waited to the count of five to see if their neighbor would pick up the phone and listen in, but he didn't hear the suspicious click indicating she had. He clicked to get the operator's attention. "Hi Mildred, please connect me to the Hollywood police division. The one that's closest to Van Ness Street."

When the duty sergeant answered, "Second Hollywood Precinct, Sergeant Noodle speaking. Who's calling?"

"This is Richard Thomas of 229 Van Ness Avenue. May I speak to Detective Jack Reardon?"

The person who answered must have said something or asked a question because Richard shook his head.

"No thank you. Could I please leave a message for Detective Reardon?"

Richard listened and nodded.

"Please have him call me back at 55521 ring 3. As soon as is convenient. Thank you, Sergeant."

"He's off for the day. He'll be on duty at 6 a.m. tomorrow." Richard stretched and yawned. "It's been a long day and I still have some reading to do for my new job." He kissed Mom on the cheek and headed for the stairs. "Thanks for dinner. That was a fun evening. And I look forward to seeing your picture in the paper tomorrow morning. Especially when the bottle bounced back."

Mom laughed along with the rest of the family. "One of my more stellar moments of fame, wouldn't you say?"

Mary Anne was the next one up the stairs after saying thanks and goodnight. And Christopher was right on her heels.

Jonathon slumped into a chair near the radio. "I'm going to listen to the radio for a while if you don't mind." He stood back up again and hugged his mother. "I'm proud of you Mom. Not every child has a mother who was graduated from M.I.T. to say the least. And then goes on to be a tool and dye designer at Lockheed. But the *piece de resistance* is having raised five amazing children." He laughed and sat back down.

Mom rumpled his hair. "I'm proud of you, Son. You've got a good head on your shoulders, just like your dad. How about we go to the beach tomorrow? We'll pack a picnic and spend the day relaxing."

"If we go, may I invite Jennifer?"

"Of course. I think of her as my third daughter."

Chapter 14

JONATHON WASN'T SURE WHAT he thought about that. He knew Jennifer was special, but he'd only dated one other girl. So how was he to know whether Jennifer really was the one for him?

And how would Mom feel if Jennifer wasn't the girl for him. Would she hate any other girl he dated?

He rubbed his hand over his head and sighed. He couldn't worry about Mom's feelings about his girlfriend. He had more important things to worry about. First off was the murder. But what could he do about that?

Better concentrate on something he could make better. Like good grades in school. His grade in Latin had slipped from almost an A, to almost a C. He had to work on that. But it was hard to concentrate on a dead language when so much else alive was going on around him. And now, speaking of dead, there was Dr. Ringwaldt. Jonathon wished he could talk to him now. Since Dad had been shipped to the Pacific to fight the Japs, their neighbor had been Jonathon's sounding board. With Dad away and Dr. R. dead, he didn't have anybody. Maybe he'd talk to his track coach.

He knew Mom would listen to him, but what did she know about guy stuff or going to war. Women didn't know about things like that.

Looking forward to shutting his thoughts off, Jonathon turned on the radio and dialed through the stations to find his favorite story station. He was just in time for the *Green Hornet*, one of his favorites. Half an hour of listening to a story and he'd be ready for bed. The story started with the Green Hornet and his trusting man servant, Cato, sneaking into the castle of this week's villain. But that was all Jonathon heard. He woke up an hour later with the radio buzzing at him, but what woke him up was the creak of the door to the den as it moved ajar.

Good Lord! he thought, *who is that?* His family were all upstairs asleep. Weren't they? *What do I do now?* he thought.

He turned slightly in the chair to look toward the den and saw a shadowy figure edge around the door. Then the figure slowly slid the door shut.

Jonathon pushed himself out of the chair and crept closer to the figure. Whoever it was certainly couldn't overwhelm Jonathon. At least not by height. The person seemed to be Mary Anne's size. But heavier.

A floorboard squeaked under Jonathon's foot and the stranger froze, looking in Jonathon's direction. What do I do now? he thought. Run? No, I let the guy know I'm big and I mean business. "Stop where you are," he said, dropping his already deep baritone almost into bass range.

The stranger looked like he was shriveling up into a ball. "I was looking for information on your neighbor, Bruno. I saw you over at his house yesterday when the police were there."

Jonathon stepped closer to the man. "Yeah, you're the guy who gave himself up when the police came."

The man nodded and Jonathon thought he trembled. "Worse day of my life," he moaned. "The coppers thought I killed Bruno." The man's voice rose in volume. "You gotta believe me. Bruno was the only friend I had. Why would I kill him?"

By now his voice had risen loud enough that Jonathon heard his family stirring upstairs. Soon, Richard, and then Mom appeared on the upstairs hallway.

"Jonathon? What's going on," Mom asked.

"I'll check," said Richard. "You go back to bed. Jonathon and I can handle this."

"I'm coming down too," said Mom, her voice having an icy edge to it.

When they got downstairs to the den door, Richard said, "I'm calling the police," and headed to the phone.

"Oh God!" the man, "I'm begging you, please don't. I couldn't stand being in their jail again. My body can't take anymore beatings." By now his voice was quivering and he reminded Jonathon of a frightened mouse.

"Why did you go with them to begin with yesterday, if you're innocent?" asked Richard.

"Yeah, and what are you doing sneaking around our house in the middle of the night?" Jonathon crossed his arms in front of his chest and glowered at the little fellow, wondering why he didn't seem to have any bruises.

Before the man could reply, Richard, said, "I'm going to check you for weaponry. Especially knives. Jonathon, hold him so he can't stab me."

Jonathon stepped toward the man, keeping a close watch on his arms and hands. He grabbed the fellow's right arm and pulled it behind his back, then he pulled the man's left arm back and held them tight. He pushed the stranger's legs apart until he wobbled.

Richard patted the intruder's torso, just the way he'd seen in the movies. He ran his hands down the inside of the man's legs and then the outside. Lastly, Richard spread his fingers and raked them through the fellow's red beard and hair.

Jonathon swallowed a laugh. *What's he going hide there, Richard?*

Richard stepped back and Jonathon released his hold on their captive.

Jonathon was beginning to feel sorry for the little fellow, but he had no business breaking into their house. "Let's all sit down and you can tell us what you're up to." He pointed to the chairs by the radio.

Mom said, "If we're going to be up so late, how about some coffee?"

"Good idea, yes please, I'd love some," chorused the three men.

"While we're waiting for the coffee, tell us who you are," said Jonathon, still feeling very manly.

"My name is Helmut Jungen. Bruno and I grew up together in Berlin." He held his hand up when Jonathon shook his head. "I know, I know. Bruno said he was born here. In Folsom to be precise. We figured that would make people accept us better."

Mom came back in the room with a pewter tray full of cups filled with coffee, and a plate of tea biscuits. Napkins, a small pitcher of milk and a bowl filled with sugar cubes was topped with sugar tongs took up the rest of the room on the tray. Each saucer had a tiny spoon nestled next to the cup.

Jonathon rolled his eyes and Richard smothered a laugh. Leave it to Mom to go hostess on them. "Mom, this man is not our guest," Richard said.

Jonathon added, "He's our prisoner."

"I don't care. I was trained to be courteous to guests in my house. Wanted or unwanted."

"My," said Mr. Jungen, "I haven't seen a coffee service since I was a boy in Berlin. My mother had a service like this that she was so proud of. I pray she's safe." A tear trickled down his cheek. "I miss her so much."

"Are you Jewish?" asked Richard. "Jungen doesn't sound Jewish."

"How can you tell that, Richard?" asked Jonathon.

Richard shrugged. "Thought Jewish names ended in 'stein'."

The man smiled a lopsided smile, "No, but my parents are small like me and my siblings, and I've heard rumors that Hitler wants to start a so-called super race."

"What does that mean?" asked Jonathon.

"He wants tall, blond people to make his idea of the new super race come true."

"Yeah, blond like him. And nobody seems to notice he's neither tall nor blond," scoffed Richard.

"Herr Hitler doesn't brook dissent," said Mr. Jungen with a sneer.

"Who sent you?" asked Mom.

Mr. Jungen stopped to stir some milk and sugar into his coffee. He took a sip and smiled. "How lovely, real coffee with real milk and sugar. What a treat."

"Answer my question, please," said Mom, her voice harsh and loud.

"And you still haven't explained your connection to our neighbor," said Richard.

Mr. Jungen put his coffee cup down, patted his mouth with his napkin and sighed. "Up until 1933 Bruno and I were in Germany working to get Hitler out of power."

"Why'd you leave home?" asked Jonathon.

"And what are you doing here?" Richard demanded.

"Were you ever in Folsom?" asked Mom.

Mr. Jungen nodded towards the boys' mother. "Yes, to learn more American ways. Bruno and I were roommates and became best friends. Then we went our separate ways. He did have a doctorate in geology from Leipzig and was already planning to come to California to study why there were so many earthquakes here.

"I became a Fuller Brush Man because I've always been a salesman. I've done pretty well selling door-to-door. My size makes me less threatening to housewives and children, and I like meeting all the people."

The small man sighed. "Bruno got in touch with me when his lovely wife died so suddenly. She was his heart and soul and he's had a hard time getting over her passing."

Mom nodded. "Yes, Bruno spoke of her often. I'm sorry we never met."

Jonathon wasn't sure their guest was telling the truth and wished his mother would stop being so polite. "Why didn't you stay in Germany, Mr. Jungen?"

"The Depression was even worse in Europe. Many Germans left home to seek a better life."

"Why don't I believe you?" asked Jonathon.

"Jonathon," said Mom, using her 'don't mess with me tone,' "don't be rude."

"No," said the man. "This is the time to be suspicious, Mrs...? Hmm. I don't seem to know your name."

"It's...," their mother said, but Richard held up his hand and shook his head. "How about you tell us what you were doing in our house uninvited first. Then perhaps we'll tell you our names."

"Of course," said Mr. Jungen. "I understand your precautions, but may I use your restroom first?" He smiled what Jonathon thought was a crocodile smile.

"I'll show you where the maid's room is, you can use the one there." Jonathon rose and beckoned for the man to precede him down the hall toward the kitchen. When they got to the tiny room with a bed, chair and desk, he stood in the bedroom and opened the door to the bathroom for Mr. Jungen. "I'll wait right here until you're done," he said, moving out of the doorway for the intruder to enter the even smaller room.

Jonathon was almost asleep on his feet when he heard the bathroom window slide open. He stepped toward the door and turned the knob. It was locked. "Mr. Jungen? Are you alright?"

There was no response and he heard to porcelain top to the water tank rattle. He pushed on the door, but it wouldn't budge. Then he heard a shoe scuffing on the wall or across the window sill. Was Mr. Jungen escaping?

Jonathon pushed harder on the door, twisting the doorknob back and forth. "Mr. Jungen, what is the matter? What are you doing?" Jonathon banged on the door. "Answer me!"

When he heard no more noise, he stepped back from the door and then charged forward, leading with his right shoulder. The door gave with the first shove, but did not open. He moved a little further back and rushed the door like a bull heading toward a matador. Crash! The door flew open with splinters of wood spewing into the air.

Richard and Mom came rushing into the room and helped Jonathon off the floor. "What in Heaven's name..." exclaimed Mom.

"Where did he go?" asked Richard.

"Out the window," and Jonathon pointed over the toilet. "Don't know what he's after, but he sure can't be trusted."

Christopher and Mary Anne, awakened by all the noise, rushed in babbling in unison. "What's all the racket? What's going on? Why's the door frame busted?"

Their mother smoothed their heads, "We had an intruder who wasn't as nice as he seemed."

Mary Anne's eyebrows slid up her forehead and Christopher asked, "What do you mean?"

"Let's go into the kitchen and try to relax." Mom took her daughter's hand and gently led her toward the kitchen table. The boys followed.

"I'll bring in the coffee service, Mom," said Jonathon. "I need to do something to settle my nerves."

"Carrying a tray full of china is not going to settle your nerves, my son. I'll get it while you tell Mary Anne and Christopher what happened."

"You remember the Studebaker we saw the other day parked at Dr. Ringwaldt's house?"

"Yeah," said Christopher, nodding his head.

"What about it?" asked Mary Anne.

"Well the man who owns it, or at least drives it, broke into our house tonight," said Richard.

"Is he a short guy with red hair and a red beard?" asked Christopher.

"How did you know that?" Jonathon's eyes got wide.

And Richard's mouth flew open.

Christopher shrugged, "He was wandering around Dr. Ringwaldt's house this afternoon when I went out to stretch my back."

"Did you talk to him at all?" Jonathon asked. "Did you tell him anything about Richard and me?"

"Well, he did ask if I knew where Dr. Ringwaldt was."

"Why would he ask that?" Jonathon wondered. "He was there yesterday when the detectives were."

"What did you say?" asked Richard.

"Just that the police took his body away."

"What was his reaction to that? Did he seem to know Dr. Ringwaldt was dead?"

Christopher shrugged. "I don't remember what he did then."

"Did you tell him anything else?" Richard's voice had a growly edge to it.

Christopher shook his head. "No, the guy seemed creepy, so I excused myself and came inside."

"Why did he seem creepy?" Mary Anne moved closer to her brothers.

Christopher shook his head. "I dunno. He just seemed too tense and he kept scanning our house."

Mom walked in and set the tray by the sink. "I wonder what he thinks we know that would tell him anything about poor Bruno," she said.

"And why did he'd break into our house?" Jonathon shook his head and raised his eyebrows again. His forehead was beginning to ache from all the times he'd been surprised in the past day. He vowed to keep his eyebrows where they should be. To calm himself, he filled the sink with hot sudsy water and washed the dishes, being as gentle as his big fingers would allow. After he rinsed each piece, Richard, who had wandered over, caressed each piece dry. Mary Anne and Christopher put the pieces away.

And Mom smiled at her brood. "I do wish your dad and Caroline were here." Then she started to cry. "And I can't believe I'll never see my father again."

All of them started to cry, even tough as nails Richard.

"Do we know any more about his funeral arrangements?" Richard looked down at his fingers and picked at a cuticle. "I'm sure I won't be able to go. What with a new job and all."

Mom shook her head. "Granny's waiting to hear back from the War Department and the Naval Academy. She wants him to buried there, even though now they want service personnel buried at Arlington Cemetery." She wiped her eyes. "I wish I could go with her, but that's too much time off from work."

Mary Anne wiped her face with her hanky. "May I go?" she asked, her voice cracking. "Granddaddy was so kind to me. And I really don't know Daddy's parents well at all. I just feel Granddaddy was special."

"That's a good idea, darling. I know Granny would love to have your company."

Jonathon winked at his sister. "What about school? You'll miss at least a week. How will you keep up with your studies?"

Mary Anne frowned and shrugged her shoulders. "Maybe they can give me the homework to take with me."

"I'll talk to the school people and arrange it all," Mom said as she stood up. She went around the circle, giving each a hug. "I love you all tremendously and am so proud to be your mother I feel like I could burst. But now I'm going to bed. Sleep in and tomorrow we'll all go to the beach. We'll have a big picnic. Invite your friends to join us, if you'd like. Goodnight my darlings."

"'Night Mom, we love you too."

Mary Anne left first, but Christopher stayed behind. Jonathon lightly punched him in the shoulder, "I'm wiped," he said. "That bed is going to feel good. I'll leave the hall light on for you, Christopher."

Richard yawned. "Just turn the lights out when you come up, Bud."

"And if you hear any strange noises or see a stranger roaming around, just holler as loud as you can." said Jonathon, winking at his now wide-eyed brother.

"Think I'll go to bed too."

Richard and Jonathon smirked. All three brothers headed up the stairs and to their rooms. But Jonathon kept startling awake during the rest of the night. Several times from creaks from the house settling. Twice from panicked thoughts about the murder of his neighbor. And once he had his earthquake nightmare again. This time his toes were hanging over the edge of the last crack before he woke up. That was it. No more sleep for him, even though his alarm clock only said five a.m.

Chapter 15

———————

HE GROANED, DRESSED AND tiptoed down the stairs. He gulped a glass of water and bit into a piece of bread.

Before he could make it past the stairs, Mom appeared from the den. "What're you doing up so early?" she asked, wiping away tears.

"Couldn't sleep. Are you okay?"

Mom nodded and tried to smile. "Just telling your father about Granddaddy. In case he hasn't heard. Hope he gets this letter."

Jonathon hugged his mother. "I'm so sorry about Granddaddy, Mom. I wish I could make it better."

Mom patted Jonathon's cheek. "You're such a good person. I'm proud of you, son.

"Thanks, Mom." Tears blurred Jonathon's eyes. He realized how scared he was. Maybe Dad was dead and nobody knew. "But are we sure Dad is okay?"

Mom let out a sob and then bit her lip. "We've got to stay strong, son. We've got to hope for the best." She patted Jonathon's cheek and forced a smile.

"I'll try." Jonathon wondered if he could be as brave as his mother. He nodded and forced a smile. "Tell Dad I miss him. Especially when I'm running."

Mom nodded. "Will do, honey. Have a nice run."

Jonathon strode across the living room to the front door. He was tempted to run a scale or two on the piano as he went by it and wake everybody up. But shook his head and grinned. *Nah, that would be mean.*

Outside, he stepped onto the grass, sat down and started his stretches. He faced with his back to Dr. Ringwaldt's house, forcing himself not think about what he'd seen.

When he felt loose, he headed toward Wilshire Boulevard, but he turned left at the first cross street, figuring he'd stop at Eddie's house to see if he wanted to go for a run. The lights were out and there was no sign of his friend. Well, he'd try on his way back.

He ran until he was relaxed and pleasantly tired, still thinking about Samantha's comment at school. *I'm going to wake Eddie up and see what was going on with the two of them.* Jonathon looked at his watch and chuckled. 6:30 a.m. was not a time that Eddie would be up if he could avoid it.

Too bad, Jonathon decided, *do him good to get up early for a change.* Something about the way Sammy's shoulders sagged, before she stiffened her spine and walked out of chemistry bothered him. And Eddie's nonchalant attitude as they walked out to track practice seemed a little forced.

Jonathon picked up some pebbles lying at the edge of the road, before walking around to the back of his friend's house. He counted three windows over until he came to Eddie's window. Two pebbles thunked into the window and Jonathon cringed, afraid he'd see the glass shatter. He hadn't meant to throw the pebbles that hard.

The glass stayed intact, but there wasn't any sign of life from inside the room. Were they home? Maybe they took a trip.

No, Eddie would have mentioned that. Jonathon threw some more pebbles and Eddie jerked the window up.

"Do you know what time it is? I'm still in bed." Eddie's chin jutted out and his mouth turned down.

"Yeah, but I want to know what's going on with you and Sammy. Come down and talk to me." Jonathon pointed to chairs on the patio.

"You are one demanding so-and-so," growled Eddie when he appeared still wearing his pajamas.

"Tell me what's going on and I'll leave you alone."

Eddie sat on a chair and shrugged his shoulders. "I don't know why she's so upset. All I did was mention that Pops and I were going to a meeting where a communist was speaking."

"You what? Why did you do that?"

"We were just curious to see if they could get us out of the depression. If they could help the poor people in our country."

"And can they?"

Eddie shook his head. "I couldn't tell, but they gave us both the willies, so we left half way through the meeting."

"Did you tell Samantha this?"

"No. She broke with me before we went to the meeting."

"Well, tell her now."

"Not sure I want to. I mean if she has so little patience with different ideas, I'm not sure I want her to be my girlfriend."

"Why does life have to be so hard?" Jonathon frowned and pulled on his forelock.

Eddie shook his head. "Don't know." He looked at Jonathon. "We done here? If so, I'm going back to bed."

Jonathon nodded. "Yeah, sleep well."

After he left his friend, he picked up his pace as he turned down Van Ness Avenue, pushing into a wind sprint. By the time he got back home, he was glistening with sweat, and ready for a quick shower.

But it was not to be. At least not at the moment, because driving toward him was at grey Studebaker with barely the top of Mr. Jungen's hat showing. What was the man doing? Maybe he was just plain crazy—looney tunes.

Jonathon hurried into his house and called the police precinct. Fortunately, it was too early in the day for Mrs. Huntsville to be on the line. "Good Morning, Hollywood Police Precinct number 2. This is Sergeant Williamson speaking."

"Yes, this is Jonathon Thomas of 229 Van Ness Avenue. Sorry to bother you so early on a Sunday, but...

"You're the next-door neighbor to the murder victim, um...oh, that's right, Dr. Bruno Ringwaldt. Is that correct?"

"Yes sir." Jonathon shivered at the tingling running down his spine. It was creepy that the policeman recognized him.

"Is there a problem?"

"Yes, there is," said Jonathon. "A very short man, I guess you could call him midget, keeps showing up looking for Dr. Ringwaldt."

"Is that the guy we had at the station yesterday?"

"Yes. He even broke into our house last night."

"Really? Did he take anything?"

"I don't know. We didn't notice anything out of place or stolen, but it was late and we didn't check thoroughly. The reason I'm calling is I just saw him driving toward our neighbor's house."

"Is he looking suspicious?"

"He was just driving up the street when I came in from my morning run."

"I'll send an officer over to check things out," said the sergeant. "That is as soon as I can. We're short-handed this morning."

"Thanks, Sergeant."

After hanging up, Jonathon headed to the kitchen where he drank two large glasses of water and ate a banana. He was headed upstairs to take a shower, but he heard the gurgle of water running through the pipes. Shoot, somebody had beaten him to the bathroom. Well, he'd just lie down for a bit until he could clean up. Hoping he wouldn't have his earthquake nightmare again.

Chapter 16

H E WOKE UP WITH a start, feeling somebody shaking his shoulder. "Hey Jonathon, Mom wanted me to see if you still plan to go to the beach with us." He opened his eyes to see Christopher looking down at him.

"Sure, sure," he said. "I was just waiting for the bathroom to be clear." Jonathon sat up and swiveled his feet to the floor. He rubbed his head. "What time is it, anyway?"

"Ten," said Christopher.

"Wow! I must have really zonked out."

"Doesn't surprise me," said Christopher. "We didn't get to bed until after one a.m. last night and you were out of here by 5:30 this morning."

"How'd you know what time I left?"

"Wasn't sleeping either."

"Tell Mom to give me ten minutes and I'll be ready. Are we skipping church today?"

"Yes."

"Oh darn, I haven't called Jennifer yet to see if she wants to go."

"Won't she go to church with her folks? I know Danny can't go. Said their dad wouldn't ever let them skip church."

Jonathon's shoulders' slumped. "You're right, Christopher. I'll just have to call her when we get back. She'll understand." At least he hoped she would.

Ten minutes later, Jonathon skipped down the steps, dressed in his bathing suit and a tee-shirt. He hadn't bothered to shave and had just run warm water over his body. Enough to rinse the dried sweat off. He was just going to get dirty at the beach. He followed his family out to the car, carrying a bag of balls so they could play catch and maybe find another group to play volleyball with.

Half an hour later, Richard pulled their big black Packard into a beach parking lot. It was the third beach they'd tried before they found the perfect one. The first beach was too narrow and too far down a cliff from the road. The second was jam packed with people already.

But this one was perfect as far as Jonathon was concerned. A deep, sandy beach and the breakers were rolling in with good height and plenty of curve to them. There were people out surfing already. All he had to do was sand his board a bit and he was good to go.

The family trundled their picnic basket, blanket, towels, beach umbrella and balls down the cliff-side trail. After they'd found the perfect spot, not too close to other people, but not too far away that they couldn't ogle the swimsuit-clad girls, they set up their camp. Mom smeared sun-blocking lotion all over herself and all over Mary Anne. The boys didn't bother with lotion. They figured they'd be in active enough to keep from getting burned. They retrieved their boards from the car's roof and rejoined their mother and sister.

Mom stood looking at the ocean. "First one in the water wins the prize!" And she ran down the beach.

"I swear Mom's a mermaid," said Richard, shaking his head.

"Yeah, I keep trying to find her seal skin," said Mary Anne and ran toward the surf line. But when she saw a guy looking at her, she slowed down and sashayed the rest of the way, giving him a dazzling grin.

"We'll have to keep an eye on our sister there, she's turning into a beauty,' said Richard.

"That she is." Christopher nodded. "All the boys ask me about whether she's interested in dating."

Richard laughed. "What do they do when you tell them Mom won't let her date yet?"

"They look disappointed, but then they pay attention to other girls. The ones with a reputation."

"We guys have one track minds," said Jonathon.

Richard smirked. "That we do and I see potential down to our left." He jerked his chin toward a group of four girls and one young woman who looked to about Richard's age. She'd already glanced his way several times.

"Time to introduce myself to that raven-haired beauty. She's got legs that won't quit." He pushed himself up off the blanket and brushed off the sand that stuck to his legs. He turned toward his brothers. "Coming?" he asked.

Christopher was up and ready in a flash, but Jonathon stayed where he sat. He shook his head. "Nah, I'd better not. Wouldn't be fair to Jennifer."

Richard looked all around his brother and shrugged. "Hmm. I don't see a leash, but it must be here some place."

"What do you mean?"

"Are you and Jennifer engaged? Married?"

Jonathon raised his eyebrows. "Huh?"

"Come on, Jonathon. I like Jennifer and think it'd be fine if you got married at some point, but you've got lots of time before that's going to happen. Doesn't mean you can't talk to other women."

Christopher nodded in agreement. He started singing "Don't Fence Me In."

Jonathon chuckled. "You're right." He stood up and they wandered down to the group of females who now sat primly on their blanket, casting sidelong glances toward the brothers.

Richard headed for the oldest of the group. He probably would have picked her even if she'd been the youngest. She was just his type with glossy jet-black hair and a long, slim body, not too heavy in the boobs department. Her eyes were a rich brown with flecks of gold showing up in the corners. She was holding a copy of William Faulkner's *Absalom!*

Absalom! Girl was smart as well as knock down gorgeous. He stood beside her and introduced himself.

"Nice to meet you, Richard. Please sit down." Her voice was throaty and silky all at the same time. "I'm Madge, and these are Christina and Carol Ann, my twin sisters" nodding at two girls who looked so much alike, Jonathon couldn't see any differences. "Lizzie and Gloria are their best friends and probably the only people in the universe who can tell which twin is which."

Gloria smiled at Jonathon and gestured for him to sit down. Her light brown hair with reddish highlights hung half way down her back accentuating her golden-brown skin. She had a beautiful smile and floored Jonathon with her slight accent. *French*, he thought.

"I'm Jonathon. Where are you from?" he asked.

She giggled and said. "I'm from Long Beach. Lived my whole life there."

"Where'd you get the accent? French, isn't it?"

"Clever boy. I spend summers in France on the Riviera. Nice, to be precise." Gloria hung her head and shuddered. "That is until Hitler invaded France. Haven't seen my father in about five years."

"That's tough. I sure miss my dad."

Christopher seemed to be hitting it off with Carol Ann, or at least that was what he was calling her. How could he tell them apart? *Maybe being a twin himself gave him a special edge.*

The brothers spent half an hour talking to the girls, making sure Lizzie and Christina were included in the conversation. Richard pulled Madge off the blanket and they strolled toward the water. Just before they reached the surf, Mom emerged out of the ocean.

Jonathon watched as Mom smiled and shook Madge's hand. Then she headed toward the family's blanket, but stopped by where Jonathon and Christopher were sitting. After they were all introduced, Mom said. "I thought we'd have lunch in about half an hour. You girls are welcome to join us." But Jonathon thought Mom was a bit cool toward Gloria, acknowledging her with the briefest nods and no offer to shake her hand.

Made him move closer to the girl. Not that he meant any disrespect toward Jennifer, it was just he didn't want Mom to determine his love life. He was only seventeen, after all.

He and Christopher helped the girls move their gear up by his family's layout. Lunch was fun and Mom, as usual, had packed enough for the whole beach. Plenty of food to go around.

Jonathon figured Gloria's family wasn't struggling to make ends meet, if she could afford to go to France every summer. Most everyone he knew had to be a little careful, though his family always seemed to have enough. And the vacations they'd taken to Yosemite were paid for by the government because of being a military family.

"Is your father in the military?" he asked Gloria.

"Yes, but he's in the French Foreign Legion somewhere in Africa. He's fighting against Rommel."

"Why is he French army?" Jonathon asked.

"Because he's French by birth. And he joined before America was in the war."

"Oh. Does he still have family over there?"

Gloria nodded. "My grandparents live south of Paris in the foothills of the
Pyrenees."

"Must be pretty there," Jonathon said, stretching out on the blanket with his arms open to the sides.

Gloria nodded and lay back next to him. "It was before the war, but Dad says the village is all shot up and the farms destroyed. Plus, my aunt and her family are prisoners somewhere in Germany." She wiped away a tear. "I have a cousin, Daphne, who's just my age. She was taken away from the family and nobody knows where." Tears streamed down Gloria's face. "She and I were very close and I don't know if I'll ever see her again."

Jonathon curved his arm around the sobbing girl and patted her shoulder. "That's awful. This war is horrible. It's causing so much pain and suffering. We just got news my grandfather died, in the Philippines."

Gloria snuggled closer. "Oh Jonathon. I'm so sorry."

They stayed together silently thinking of their missing and dead relatives.

Jonathon drifted off to sleep.

The beach sirens howled and the lifeguards whistled for everyone to hide in the dunes at the base of the cliffs. When they hunkered down in the dunes, Christopher pointed out to sea where low flying planes were headed right for them. "Are those Zeros?" he shouted. "They look like Zeros!" He moved closer to the dune.

"Duck!" yelled Mary Anne. She rolled herself into the smallest ball she could and Mom curled herself around her daughter.

As best he could, Jonathon huddled himself around Gloria who'd tucked Lizzie in front of her.

Richard gathered the other girls in front of them, as the planes strafed the beach. One child down the beach screamed in agony, his mother screaming "No!"

Coastal batteries opened fire and other planes—American planes— zoomed in from above. A Zero burst into flames and spiraled into the ocean. Those on the beach who saw the plane crash, cheered and shouted "Kill them all!"

Just as soon as the battle had started it was over, the remaining Jap planes veering back to sea.

"Hope they all run out of fuel and drown in the ocean," growled Jonathon. "Killing a little child like that."

But then he remembered a comment Jennifer had made last week when Eddie had talked about killing all Japs and Krauts. She said, "What did their kids do to us? Should they die?"

Gloria shook him awake. "Are you alright? You were twitching and then you started muttering about somebody named Jennifer in your sleep."

Jonathon jerked up. "Oh, I was dreaming about the war. I dreamt the Japs were flying overhead and shooting at us. And then I remembered a comment my girlfriend made about this war not being the children's fault and that we should not hate anybody but the people who started it.

Gloria shoved him away. "Girlfriend?"

Chapter 17

"**Y**OU HAVE A GIRLFRIEND?" asked Gloria, moving further away from him. "How come this is the first I'm hearing about her?" She stood up and crossed her arms in front of her chest.

"Um. I guess I just forgot to tell you. It's not like we're engaged or anything."

Gloria stepped closer to her friends. "Sorry to break up the party, but I'd like to just go home, please."

Her friends looked up in surprise. "Okay?" said Lizzie, raising her eyebrows.

"What's going on here?" asked Madge.

"Up until now Jonathon failed to mention he has a girlfriend."

Richard stood up. "He didn't mean to be sneaky. He doesn't have a sneaky bone in his body. I guess he just didn't think it was relevant." He looked down at Madge who was getting up from the blanket. But when he extended a hand to help her up, she turned away.

"Come on Madge. Don't be mad at me. It was just a misunderstanding. Let's play volley ball and forget about it."

But Madge reached down to gather her stuff.

After thanking Mom, the other girls turned to Jonathon. "Thanks for ruining our day," they said in unison and headed to their car.

Richard reached for Madge's hand. "I really would like to see you again. Can't I have your phone number?"

Madge slowly pulled her hand away. "You know my name. If you're serious, look our family up in the phone book." She turned toward her friends with a slow shake of her head but she turned back to Richard. "I might talk to you."

Richard scowled at Jonathon.

"Good going, Jonathon," said Christopher. "I was having a good time."

Jonathon hung his head and picked at the blanket. "Sorry everybody, didn't mean to ruin our day."

"I'm sorry you hurt Gloria's feeling, Jonathon, but she'll get over it." Mom stood up and grabbed her towel. "And you didn't ruin my day." She looked down at her watch sitting on top of the blanket. "It's been an hour since we ate, so is anybody else ready for a swim? Then we'll pack up and head home."

Mom and Mary Anne splashed and swam for half an hour while Jonathon, Richard and Christopher surfed the growing waves. Riding the waves soothed Jonathon's emotions. Was he wrong to sit with Gloria? Did he lead her on? Was he cheating on Jennifer? No, he decided, he was just having fun at the beach. He wasn't even sure it was worth mentioning to her.

Clouds rolled in just as they were packing up for the ride home. "Perfect timing," commented Mary Anne.

"Let's hope the rain holds off until we're in the house," said Richard. "This car doesn't have the best windshield wipers."

But three minutes into the drive they had to slow to a crawl as the rain poured down making Richard stick his head out the window to see the road. Lightning forked out the sky like an enormous snake and thunder rocked the car.

"Maybe we should pull over until the storm passes," suggested Mom, with a death grip on the passenger-side door handle.

"No, I'm afraid people won't see us."

"I think I see clear sky ahead." Jonathon craned his head out the window and up. He pulled his head back in and wiped his face. "'Course I just got an eyeful of rain."

Christopher looked at his brother and grinned.

Mary Anne laughed and said, "Serves you right for cheating on Jennifer."

"I didn't cheat on anybody," protested Jonathon. "I was just passing the time."

Richard laughed, "You're not going to win this one, brother mine. Best just ride it out."

They all laugh at that, and when the rain let up, Richard picked up speed. Finally, they made it home under a clear sky and bright sunshine. But something seemed strange about their street.

"Why are those police cars parked in our driveway?" Mom peered through the windshield.

"Mr. Jungen's car is there also," said Jonathon. "He sure is strange."

"He gives me the creeps," said Mary Anne, her shoulders shuddering.

Richard parked the car on the street, since their driveway was full of police cars. He led his family toward the first patrol car, but his friend Jack, wearing his badge on his shirt, stepped in front of him.

"Hold on, buddy. There's been another murder."

"In Dr. Ringwaldt's house?"

"No," said Jack's partner as he moved up to the family. "In your house."

"Our house!" exclaimed Jonathon. "Why would someone be murdered in our house?"

"That's what we'd like to know," said the older policeman.

"Who is it?" asked Richard.

"We don't know yet," answered Jack.

"It's not the midget is it?" asked Jonathon. "He broke into our house last night."

The policemen stared at him. "And why are we just now hearing about this?" asked Jack.

"I tried to call you last night, but the desk sergeant said you weren't on duty. Said he'd give you the message," Richard replied.

Both officers shook their heads, "Didn't hear a word from him," said the older police man. "Why did the midget break in?"

"We don't know," answered Richard and Jonathon at the same time.

Jonathon pointed at the grey Studebaker. "He must be around here somewhere. That's his car."

"He's not in your house," said Jack.

"Hmm," said the older policeman. "I haven't seen him and this guy is bigger than Jonathon."

"Good Heavens," said Mom, joining the group.

"I'm sorry to say, but one of you is going to have identify the body. He doesn't have any identification on him."

"I want you all to stay outside while I go see if I know this man," said Mom.

"I'll go," said Richard. "I'm getting into this line of work anyway."

"We'll go together," answered Mom her voice growly, making Jonathon think of a cat protecting its territory. Richard and Mom followed the policemen into the house.

"What's going on? Why are all those people wanting to break into our house?" asked Mary Anne.

"Yeah, it's exciting, isn't it?" said, Christopher.

His twin scowled at him. "I don't think so. Gives me the willies."

"I agree with Mary Ann." Jonathon headed toward the front of the house. "Maybe we can take a look in through the front windows."

"Good idea," said Christopher.

"I think I'll stay here. I'm not keen on seeing a dead person in our house." Mary Anne shivered and hugged her arms around her middle.

All the two boys could see was a sea of policemen hovering around the door to the den. And then everybody headed toward the front door, two men pushing a gurney in front of them with a covered body strapped to it. At least Jonathon assumed it was a body. What else could it be?

Richard held Mom's arm to steady her as they followed the procession of police out the door. Her face glowed ivory white and she was shaking.

"That was our neighbor, Mr. Schmidt," said Richard rubbing his hand across his face. "I wonder how many more of our neighbors are involved in this?"

Jonathon shook his head. "Are we safe here? And why are these people breaking into our house?"

"The police don't want us to stay here for a while. They need to search our house to see if they can find some evidence." Mom looked around her. "Where's Mary Anne?"

"I'll get her," said Christopher, pointing toward the street. "She's by our car."

"In the meantime, you boys go pack enough clothes for three days. And pack your school supplies as well. We may be staying away from home for a few days, but you'll still be studying." Mom shook her head and sighed. "Hope I don't lose my job over this."

"No ma'am," said one of the policemen, "We'll tell them it's a national security issue."

"Will they believe that?" asked Richard.

The policeman nodded. "We've got connections."

"Richard, please help me get the suitcases and put them in your rooms," said Mom.

"Mom said we've got to pack and get out of here in half an hour," said Jonathon after Christopher escorted Mary Anne up from their car.

"Where are we going?" asked Mary Anne.

"Wilshire Boulevard Plaza."

"That's a fancy hotel. Do we have to wear our best clothes?" asked Christopher.

"No, just your regular clothes," said Jonathon. "But we can't tell anybody where we're going."

"Except Granny, right?" asked Mary Anne.

"Yeah," said Christopher. "She's supposed to move in with us, isn't she?"

"Ooh, I wonder if Mom remembers that." Mary Anne frowned.

Jonathon nodded. "We'd better ask her." He shook his head. "Poor Mom, I wonder how much more she's going to have to deal with."

When they got inside, Mom and Richard were just coming out of the kitchen with the suitcases. Everybody grabbed one and started up the stairs.

"Um, Mom?" Christopher asked, "we hate to bring up more problems, but have we told Granny about our move?"

"Drat," said Mom. "I forgot. She's moving out of her apartment tomorrow. I wonder where she should stay? I don't want to put her in harm's way."

Mom sat down on the stairs and cradled her head with her hands. She leaned into Richard, who'd sat down beside her.

"Maybe the policeman can do something about it," said Jonathon about ready to cry himself.

"Good idea, son," Mom said, standing and heading up the stairs. "I'll ask, but now let's just get our things and leave. Oh, and remember your bathing suits. I believe the hotel has a swimming pool."

The family headed to their bedrooms and folded their clothes into the suitcases Mom gave them to use. "Remember your toothbrushes and other bathroom supplies. And, Christopher, remember clean undergarments."

Richard raised his hand to stop everybody from going to their rooms. "Remember, and this is important, we cannot tell anyone where we're going." He looked at Jonathon. "That includes Jennifer."

"Wow, you're getting too big for your britches there, brother. You may have a job now, but you're not my boss."

Mom reached over and stroked Jonathon's arm. "I think we're all edgy now, but Richard does have a point. No one should call anyone." She looked at Mary Anne and Christopher. "That includes your best friends."

At the required time, the family was downstairs, ready to go. A solid-looking policeman came in through the maid's entrance. "We're taking you out this way," he said. "It's the least visible door." They all traipsed through the kitchen, past the walk-in pantry and laundry room and out the door that led to the side of the rose garden. Three unmarked police cars were parked in the driveway. Jonathon always wondered why the police thought their unmarked cars looked like anything other than police cars. How many cars had those big spotlights mounted by the front window? Other than police cars, not many.

The policeman Jonathon had nicknamed Officer Fullback opened the back door to the last car in the line. "Mrs. Thomas and Mary Anne, get in this one and lie down on the floorboards."

Mom looked at him with raised eyebrows and crossed arms. "On the floor?"

"We don't want people to know you've left. We don't know if anybody is watching your house, but it seems a good possibility."

"Mom," said Mary Anne as she got into the car, "remember to tell them about Granny."

"That's right, thanks honey." She turned toward Officer Fullback. "My mother is due to leave her apartment tomorrow and move in with us. Here are her address and telephone number. Should she come with us to the hotel?"

Officer Fullback shrugged his shoulders. "I don't know the answer, but we'll arrange something."

After Mom and Mary Anne were as comfortably as possible hidden on the floor of the first car, a detective got in the front seat and the driver backed out of the driveway, heading off toward Wilshire Boulevard.

Christopher started toward the second car in line, but Officer Fullback, stopped him. "We're going to wait fifteen minutes before you go."

"Why's that?" asked Jonathon.

"We don't want anyone to see a pattern to the cars leaving."

"So, if you leave at different times, the neighbors will think you're finishing up your investigative tasks separately?"

Officer Fullback nodded. "That's the hope."

Fifteen minutes later with Richard and Christopher ensconced on the floor of the second car, the driver backed out and headed to the right.

Ten minutes later, Officer Fullback said, "Okay, Jonathon, put your suitcase on the back seat, but don't get in."

Jonathon turned to stare at the policeman. "What am I supposed to do now?"

"I want you to walk away from your house and go see Jennifer. I'll pick you up a block from her house after you've had half an hour with her."

Jonathon turned to walk down the driveway, but Officer Fullback stopped him. He pointed to the door they'd come out of. "Go back inside and go out the front door. And remember. Do not say a word to her about what's going on."

"What do I tell her?"

"Tell her you're sorry you couldn't take her to the beach with your family." The policeman shrugged. "Or something along those lines."

Jonathon wondered how the guy knew they'd been to the beach. Instead he asked, "Do I say we're staying at a hotel for a few days and I won't be in school?"

"Tell her you think you're coming down with something."

"Won't she think it strange that I came to visit her, if I'm supposed to be sick?"

"You'll think of something," said Officer Fullback with a flip of his hand.

Jonathon did as he was told, walking down the block thinking about his meeting Gloria. Should he tell Jennifer about that? Or tell her about his dream instead? Yeah, that's what he'd do.

But when he got to her house, her younger brother, Danny, answered the door. "Hey Jonathon, you're in trouble with Jennifer."

Jonathon's eyebrows shot up. "What did I do? I didn't think we had plans for today and Mom decided we'd go to the beach. I was going to invite your family to come along, but I knew your dad wouldn't let you skip church. Please tell her I'm sorry I missed her."

"She was fine until Kurt came over to see if she wanted to go to a movie. When she said she was waiting for you, he told her he'd heard you were at the beach snuggling with some hot girl.

Jonathon's mouth snapped closed and he said, "I wasn't snuggling with her!"

Danny shrugged. "Don't tell me. Tell Jennifer. Anyway, she went to the movies with Kurt and some of his friends."

"Geeze. Guess I goofed, huh?" Jonathon hung his head. "Hope I can fix this."

Was Jennifer losing interest in him. Kurt kept showing up next to her. He glanced at his watch and realized he still had fifteen minutes before he was going to meet Officer Fullback. Maybe he'd grill Danny about how much time Kurt and Jennifer were spending together. She did tutor him on English since he still spoke German at home.

He turned back just as Danny was shutting the door. "Hey Danny, could I trouble you for a drink of water? I got kind of thirsty walking over here."

"Sure, come on in. Dad just bought a big pitcher to keep in the icebox. We fill it with ice and water every morning, so it ought to be nice and cold by now." Danny poured of them each a large glass of water and the two boys settled in at the table in the breakfast nook.

"I've always liked this nook," said Jonathon. "It seems like such a nice place to have breakfast."

Danny nodded. "I like to do my homework here, or just sit and read. The sunlight makes it seem so cheery, but I also like how cozy it feels in the evening."

"Speaking of homework, how much time does Jennifer spend tutoring Kurt?" Jonathon winked. "I mean, should I be worried?"

Danny smiled and shook his head. "Nah, Jennifer says she feels sorry for him. He seems so homesick for Germany."

Jonathon nodded, "I guess I'd be homesick if I had to leave my country. It's gotta be hard to have to learn a new language in a strange place. I know it's hard enough to make new friends every couple of years when Dad is transferred."

Danny nodded. "I can understand the homesick part, but Jennifer says he kinda scares her too."

"Why?"

"She says he tries to order her around all the time. He keeps telling her a woman should obey her man."

"That's weird. Must be a German thing." Jonathon smiled. "Still, I guess a lot of guys in this country think a woman should stay at home and raise the family. It's never been that way in my family. I mean since we move so often Mom's never had a paying job, but she always manages to find volunteer work."

Danny grinned. "On the other hand, you'd better come up with a good explanation for why you were snuggling with that girl at the beach today."

"I wasn't cuddling! I was comforting her." Jonathon looked at Danny and frowned. "This isn't going to be easy is it? And I still don't know how Kurt knew I was at the beach."

Jonathon glanced at this watch. *Probably time to meet up with the policeman*, he thought. He finished his water, and put the glass in the kitchen sink. "Thanks for the water, Danny. Tell Jennifer I'll try to call later this evening."

He headed in the direction Officer Fullback had indicated. But after he had walked three blocks with no sign of the police car, he sat on a bus-stop bench to think. Then, almost as if someone had slapped him on the back of his head, he remembered that just last week he and Dr. Ringwaldt had traded baseball cards. Dr. R had given him one of Babe Ruth's last year in the sport. It had something hand written on it.

Chapter 18

E'D TELL OFFICER FULLBACK, if the guy ever showed up. Jonathon stood up. *Maybe he'd head for the hotel. But what hotel was it? Something Plaza? Oh, Wilshire Plaza.*

How many blocks up Wilshire was it? He knew he'd passed it on one of his runs, but which way had he turned to get to it? Well, he'd go to Wilshire and turn right. If he hadn't come to it after ten blocks, he'd cross the street and head back toward Van Ness. He wondered if he'd be noticed walking back and forth? *Wasn't the object to not leave a trail?*

After five blocks, a dark blue Nash pulled up beside him. "Hey stranger," said the driver.

Jonathon jumped back and was about to run when he realized who the driver was. "Oh, I didn't recognize you."

"Happens to me all the time," said Officer Fullback. "Big as I am, you'd think I'd be easy to spot." He smiled and beckoned to the passenger-side door.

Jonathon got in the car and the policeman headed up the Boulevard. "It's about a mile up the road on the left. Let me fill you in on your new name. You are now Philip Magillacuddy."

"Philip? What happened to Jonathon?"

"We don't want to people to find you, so we gave you a new name."

"What does any of this have to do with me and my family? I mean, why are we involved?"

"Well, you did find one neighbor's body. You've had two different people break in and one person die in your house."

"Yeah, but we had nothing to do with Dr. Ringwaldt or Mr. Schmidt's deaths."

"Probably not," said the policeman.

"What do you mean, 'probably not'?" Jonathon squirmed in his seat. How could anybody think they were involved?

"Well, doesn't it seem strange to you that all these people who live around you keep being murdered. Or breaking into your house?"

"It's only been two people killed. Yeah...I guess so, or maybe it's just a coincidence?"

"Could be, but we gotta check it out. In any case, we thought it'd be a good idea to keep you safe." Officer Fullback stuck out his left arm to signal a left turn and pulled into the hotel's driveway.

"Geeze," said Jonathon, "with a name like Plaza, you'd think this would a classier place," as he peered at the dirty front door and stained cement siding.

"Hey, it may not be the Ritz, but it's clean inside and nobody's going to look for you in a joint like this."

He stopped by the front door and put his car in neutral. "Do you remember your name?"

"Sure, it's Jonathon Thomas."

The policeman looked at Jonathon as if he were an idiot. "Hey kid, pay attention. Your name is Philip Magillacuddy."

"Oh yeah, I forgot."

"Well, don't. Here's your key, your room number is 306 right next to your mother and sister, who are now Aunt Ginger and cousin Felicity."

"Philip Magillacuddy lives in room 306. Gotcha."

"Don't bother talking to the clerk at the front desk. Just smile as you go by."

Jonathon nodded, and after grabbing his suitcase out of the back seat, headed inside.

He stopped, remembering he wanted to tell the policeman about the Babe Ruth card. But Officer Fullback had already pulled onto Wilshire Boulevard.

He was about to head toward the elevator, when the desk clerk called out. "Hey Philip, your brothers asked you to meet them at Jimmy's diner. You know the one? Corner of Wilshire and Henry. About four blocks down on the left? It looks like a street car."

"Okay, but I'll put my suitcase in our room first."

The fellow shook his head, "No time. I'll hold it for you behind my desk."

"Thanks, but I'd like to go freshen up first."

"Suit yourself," said the clerk, pinching his mouth closed and pointing the way to the elevator.

When Jonathon—oh that's right he had to start thinking of himself as Philip—got to the hotel room, he heard the radio playing a Billy Holliday tune, "Strange Fruit." But it was odd to hear the radio. Was it coming from a different room? He put the key in the lock and turned the knob. Richard and Christopher looked up and smiled.

"Where you been?" asked Richard.

"We were beginning to worry," chimed in Christopher.

"I got lost." He raised his eyebrows. "The desk clerk said I was supposed to meet you Jimmy's diner. What are you doing here?"

Christopher looked puzzled and Richard shook his head. "We never told him that."

"That's strange. Wonder why he did that." Jonathon sat on the cot set by the interior door. "This mine?"

His brothers nodded, "Last in, last served," said Christopher. He stuck out his hand, "Oh by the way, I'm Jacob."

Richard smiled, "And I'm Charles."

"Sure hope I remember this." Jonathon shook hands with his brothers and pointed at the connecting door. "Philip," he pointed at his chest, "would like to know if he still has a mother and sister."

"Nice to meet you, Philip," said Richard and shook his head. "No mother or sister, but we do have a very nice aunt by marriage and her daughter. You remember Aunt Ginger, don't you? She's Uncle Leon's wife. And, of course you remember cousin Felicity."

Jonathon rolled his eyes. "Oh yeah."

"We were waiting for you to show up. We're hungry," said Christopher.

"Knock on Aunt Ginger's door there. I'm sure she and Felicity would like to go to dinner with us," said Richard.

"Are you two worried about keeping our names straight?" Jonathon asked, as he knocked on the door. "Mom, uh Aunt Ginger, it's Philip. We're going to get a bite to eat. Would you and uh, uh, Felicity like to come?"

Mom opened the door. "Where have you been? I was getting worried."

"The police wanted it to seem as if at least someone was home at our house. They had me walk away as if I was going to see Jennifer."

"Well, I'm starving," said Mary Anne. "Let's go eat."

"Shall we ask the desk clerk if he knows of a good place close by?" suggested Mom.

Jonathon shook his head, "I wouldn't ask that guy the time of day."

When Mom opened her mouth to comment, Richard said, "We'll tell you later, but let's go to that diner he mentioned."

When Jonathon started to protest, Richard said, "I want to see what's going on there."

Mom's quizzical look prompted Christopher to say, "We'll tell you while we're eating."

When they got down to the lobby, the desk clerk Jonathon had talked with was nowhere to be seen. Instead a taller, curly headed fellow nodded at them pleasantly from behind the desk. "Have a nice evening," he said.

Jonathon opened his mouth to ask where the other guy was, but Richard grabbed his arm and shook his head.

When they got outside and away from the hotel, Richard said, "There's something fishy going on here. I don't think we can trust anybody."

"Not even the police?" asked Mary Anne.

"Surely we can trust the police," said Mom.

Richard shrugged and shook his head. "I really don't know."

They walked on in silence. Jonathon slipped sidelong glances at other people walking along around them and riding by in cars. One man in a grey rain jacket seemed to be walking just a few steps behind, but keeping up. Was that just happenstance? Or was he tailing them? If so why? To protect them?

His shoulders tightened more with every step and he could feel his neck start to cramp. Then he thought he saw a grey Studebaker behind them. He shook his head and sighed with relief when they got to the diner.

Chapter 19

A S THEY HAD AT the Brown Derby, they found a big, curved booth so they could all sit comfortably together. The diner was busy, and the aroma of bacon and cheese grilling, plus hamburgers and hot dogs made Jonathon's mouth water. He looked to see if he could see any vegetables cooking. Mom would not be happy if she couldn't have green vegetables.

He looked around the restaurant and saw only what appeared to be businessmen having lonely meals or families having fun. Two couples at different tables sat close to each other and shared a plate of food. Nobody seemed to be paying their family any mind.

"Why do you suppose that desk clerk wanted me to come here?" he asked his brothers. "He didn't even want me take my suitcase up to our room."

"What are you talking about, Jonathon?" Mom asked.

"Aunt Ginger," said Richard, looking sternly at Mom. "Either the guy was playing games with Philip, or he knows who we are."

"I don't get it," said Jonathon. "How could he know who we are?"

"Did you get a look at his nametag?" asked Christopher.

"Why?" asked Jonathon.

"To see if he had a German last name."

Jonathon shook his head. "Didn't occur to me."

Mary Anne put her finger to her mouth and hissed out a shushing sound, as the waitress approached. She smiled when the woman got to the table. "I'm famished," she said and ordered a cheeseburger, fries and a strawberry milk shake. And, after a stern look from Mom, she added a small green salad.

Everyone else ordered basically the same thing, except for what to drink. Water and no fries for Mom, sodas for Richard and Jonathon, and a root beer float for Christopher.

Since nobody was in the booth next to them as far as Jonathon could see, the family felt more comfortable talking about their problems.

"How long do we have to stay in the hotel?" asked Jonathon.

Mom said, "The police estimated around three or four days. They'd thought they'd have things wrapped up by then."

"They don't seem to know who's doing what, seems to me," muttered Jonathon.

Christopher and Mary Anne nodded in agreement, but Richard said, "I don't know. Jack says they are thinking that Dr. Ringwaldt and Mr. Schmidt were maybe part of some secret group."

"What kind of group?" asked Mom.

"Nazi spies?" asked Christopher forgetting to close his mouth.

"I can't imagine either one of those men being Nazis," said Jonathon. "And what does Mr. Jungen have to do with this? He's the one who keeps popping up all over." He looked around the diner. "I even thought I saw his Studebaker following us along the street as we were walking here."

"Mr. Jungen seemed like such a nice fellow. I can't imagine he's involved in anything nefarious," said Mom.

"Then why did he sneak into and out of our house yesterday?" asked Jonathon.

"I don't know, but it must have been something we did to frighten him," Mom answered.

"Oh boy," said Mary Anne, "here comes our food. I've not had anything to eat since the beach." The minute the waitress put down the strawberry milkshake, Mary Anne stuck the straw in her mouth and slurped down a third of the liquid.

Mom scowled and said, "This may be just a greasy spoon, young lady, but that doesn't mean we have to forget our manners."

Christopher, who was just about to sip his float, put his hand back in his lap.

"Well, I can see we're all hungry." Mom nodded to waitress when the food was all served. "Thank you."

She took a bite of her salad and the family all began to eat. Silence reigned for a few minutes.

Mary Anne finished her milkshake and patted her stomach. "Now I'm happy."

"You haven't finished your fries," said Christopher. "Can I have them?"

"I believe you mean, may not can," said his sister, with a smug smile on her face. "And no, you may not. I'm going to nibble on them until everyone else is done."

"Let's debate this question of 'may' versus 'can'. Yes, Christopher is capable of eating the fries, if given the chance. But are you willing to give him the chance? If not, then he may not eat them," said Richard.

Mom was strict on manners, but Dad, when he was home, was just as strict on proper grammar. They'd all learned to sit up straight at in a chair and not slouch. And, they'd all learned when to say who and when to say whom. Still, Jonathon wanted to discuss the mess the family was in instead of correct grammar.

"Are you going to work tomorrow, Mom?"

"No, but the police are making up an excuse for me, so I won't lose my job."

"How about you, Richard? You're supposed to start your new job tomorrow. I can't imagine your boss being happy about your not showing up."

"I was planning on going in."

"Under what name? And if you go under your new name, won't they say you're not the one they hired?"

"Good question, Jonathon. Oops, I guess I mean Philip. Blast! This is too hard. I'll pay the bill and let's go back to the hotel, so we can talk this out."

The family stepped outside while Richard paid and Jonathon glanced around for suspicious looking people or cars. There was a fellow leaning against a store front across the street from them, with his right leg propped up on the wall. His face was partially concealed as he lit a cigarette and he seemed to be paying nobody any attention. Down the street, heading their direction was a grey car, but Jonathon couldn't see if it was a Studebaker. He felt his shoulders and spine tightening and he wonder if he would go mad from the stress he sensed.

"Easy Jonathon," said Mom patting his arm, "I know you're on edge, but try to think of good things. It's the only way to get through this mess."

"Philip is fine, thank you Aunt Ginger, but my friend Jonathon is scared silly. He's sure either the world or he is going explode."

"I'm glad you're fine Philip. Tell your friend he's right to be scared, dear. But why don't you let me worry about all this. You just take care of you." Mom rubbed her hand up and down his back.

"How can I do that, when I can't even remember who I am anymore? And what are all my friends going to think? And how are they not going to run into me? And how am I going to keep my grades up, when I'm not going to school?"

Mom shrugged her shoulders and shook her head. "I can't give you the answers to your questions. But I have faith we'll sort this out."

"We do have our school work with us," said Mary Anne. A policeman dropped it off at the hotel."

"Wonder what they told the school," said Christopher.

Richard joined them then, slipping his wallet into his pants pocket. "All set. Let's head back to the hotel."

Jonathon realized he wasn't the only one in the family looking to see if people were following them or, at least looking them suspiciously.

Christopher peered into every alley they passed.

Mary Anne turned her head every time someone passed them on the street to see if the person looked back. Some of them did, but she couldn't tell if it was because she'd look at them first.

Richard's head turned to watch the cars that went by them.

Mom twitched her fingers and arms every time someone came too close to her.

Jonathon was glad for the help, because he was sure he couldn't see everything. He wondered if the cops were still keeping a watch over them. But mainly he wondered how'd they gotten into this mess to begin with. And why were Dr. Ringwaldt and Mr. Schmidt dead? What had they done and to whom? And what did his baseball cards have to do with anything? Was it maybe that writing on the Babe Ruth card? Did other of his cards have extra writing on them that he just hadn't noticed?

Then, across the street, he saw a grey Studebaker parked across the street, with little puffs of smoke spewing out the tailpipe. He poked Richard's ribs and said, "slowly turn your head and see if you see anybody in that Studebaker."

Richard reached down as if to pick up something from the sidewalk. He turned his head slightly and then stood up, pinching his fingers as if he were holding a coin in his hand. "I couldn't see anybody. But the car's motor is running so somebody has to be there. Or maybe in that tobacco store and left his car on."

Christopher had stopped ahead of them and started back.

But Jonathon shook his head and hissed, "Just keep walking." He looked back toward the street just as a tall, heavy-set, bald man placing his hat back on his head exited the tobacco store, a cigar clenched between his teeth.

The man started toward the Studebaker, glancing in Jonathon's direction before opening the passenger-side door, ducking inside and slamming the door shut. With a grind of gears the car moved out in to traffic. How many short people in L.A. drove grey Studebakers? Couldn't be that many, but the car didn't make a U turn to come in Jonathon's direction. Maybe Mr. Jungen was just driving somewhere with a friend.

Jonathon lengthened his stride, pulling his brothers along with him. He gave Mom and Mary Anne a glance as he passed and beckoned with his chin that they should move more quickly. Mary Anne took Mom's hand and they sped up a bit.

Mom looked at her watch as they passed a street light. "We'd best hurry back to our hotel, before we get arrested for violating the curfew."

The whole family stretched their strides, trying vainly to keep up with Jonathon. Soon they were at the hotel door and when Richard pulled it open, they all sighed in relief.

Jonathon checked to see who was behind the counter. This time, it was a completely new clerk. "How many clerks work here?" Jonathon asked the fellow.

"What do you mean, sir? Just the day clerk, who left at eight and the night clerk, me."

"Did the day clerk get sick during his shift and have to be relieved?"

"No, not that I'm aware of. George was here when I got in. And he's usually on duty."

"Must be my mistake," said Jonathon, "thought I saw another person when I first came in this afternoon." He smiled and waved as the family all moved toward the elevator.

"Wait!" said the clerk. "I just remembered something George said."

The family stopped at the elevator doors and turned in the clerk's direction.

"He said he'd gone to restroom. That he was in there about five minutes, but he couldn't get back out. He said the door was locked or jammed. Something was keeping it from opening."

"What did he do?" asked Mary Anne.

"He had to ram it with the trash can to break the lock."

Chapter 20

WHEN THEY WERE SAFELY in their rooms, with the connecting door open, Jonathon said, "There's something strange going on here. I know there was a different person behind the desk at first. The guy who tried to get me to go to Jimmy's, but leave my suitcase at the front desk." He clenched and unclenched his fists. "How would anybody know we were here?"

"Wonder if the fellow you saw locked George in the bathroom." Richard rubbed his hand over his face.

Christopher asked, "Do you think the police are setting us up?"

"Why would they do that?" Mary Anne's eyebrows rocketed up toward her hairline.

"Are we safe anywhere?" asked Richard, slapping his bed covers.

"Maybe we should call the police. I have a special number to call if we have problems," said Mom.

"Where are we going to call from? Not this hotel if we think we're being spied on." Jonathon stood up from his cot and headed toward the door.

"Where are you going, Son?" asked Mom.

"Give me the phone number and I'll go down the street to the Woolworths I saw. They've probably got a pay phone." Jonathon held out his hand.

"You're not going alone." Mom said, standing in front of the door.

"Why not? I can walk in the shadows. No one will see me."

"What about the curfew?" asked Christopher.

Jonathon looked at his watch. "We've got about twenty minutes."

"That ought to be enough time," Richard said.

"It's too dangerous. Maybe two of us should go." Mary Anne positioned a chair by the door, sitting so her legs blocked access.

"I'm less conspicuous alone, because I don't seem as big if there's no-one to compare me to."

Richard nodded his head. "I think Jonathon's right." He held up his hand to stop Mom from speaking. "But I think he does need protection. I'll tail him."

Mom frowned. "I don't want anything else to happen to us."

"We're not safe now," said Christopher.

"I'll be careful and Richard will watch my back." Jonathon pasted a smile on his face.

"Well, I guess it'll be alright." Mom sighed. "But you boys be very careful," she said as she handed Jonathon the paper with the special number and four nickels. "That ought to give you enough time for the call."

"We will be fine," Jonathon said hoping it was true. He turned to Richard. "I saw a sign in the lobby pointing to a side door. I'll go that way. You wait three minutes and follow me out the front door."

Richard smiled. "Good idea, but I'm going talk to the desk clerk now to distract him. That way maybe he won't see you leave."

Jonathon walked down the stairs after Richard took the elevator. His brother was deep in conversation with the clerk when Jonathon slipped out the side door. He turned to his right, then to his right again and walked in front of the entrance.

Richard was heading toward the front door, blocking the clerk's view of it.

Jonathon stayed as close to the side of the buildings as he could, several times scraping his elbow on the bricks, but he felt as if no-one could see him. He hoped his brother was able to keep enough distance to not give Jonathon away, but close enough to come to his rescue.

The pay phone inside the Woolworth's was up near the cashier's booth, though out of her line of sight. Jonathon slipped a nickel into the slot and jumped at the loud pinging noise. When he got the connection hum, he dialed the number. He glanced over at the clerk to see if she was paying attention to him, but she was still reading her movie magazine and snapping her gum.

With each ring of the phone, Jonathon's shoulders pinched tighter together. Finally, after seven rings, a voice growled, "Detective Bill Cumpler speaking. What do you want?"

Jonathon said, "May I please speak with Detective Jack Reardon? This is Jonathon Thomas, otherwise known as Philip…"

"Yeah, yeah, I know who you are. I'll see if he's still here." He put the phone down and Jonathon heard him walking off. The clock on the store wall clicked the minutes going by.

"Anybody seen Jack? He's got a phone call."

"Please deposit another nickel," said the operator.

"Yes ma'am," said Jonathon, and clinked his second nickel into the slot. He wondered if the operator was listening in. Another minute went by and Jonathon was beginning to worry that he would run out of money, when he heard the clump of shoes walking on a hard wood floor.

"Officer Reardon speaking. What can I help you with?"

"Jack, this is Jonathon. Oops I'm mean Philip Magillacuddy. We've got a question about the hotel we're staying in. We're not sure it's safe." Jonathon told him the story of the desk clerk trying to get his suitcase.

"Please deposit another nickel," came the bored voice of the operator.

Jonathon slipped in his next to last nickel. "I've got to hurry, I only have one more nickel."

"Go back to the hotel and gather your stuff," said Jack. "We'll send a taxi to pick you up. The bill's already paid for the night."

"When will you get there?"

"'Bout half an hour."

Jonathon hung up and nodded to the cashier on his way out the door. He hurried back to the hotel. The clerk looked up in surprise when he came through the front door, but Jonathon just waved and headed to elevator. He was in the room with his mother and siblings, when Richard came in.

Twenty minutes later, the clerk knocked on the door. When Christopher open it, the perplexed man said, "There's a taxi cab waiting for you." He looked at the bags and asked, "Is something wrong with your rooms? We thought you were staying for several days."

"Nothing wrong, thank you. We've just had a change of plans."

The clerk still stood there, blocking the doorway.

"We're all paid up, correct?" asked Mom.

"We'd best not keep the cabbie waiting," said Richard.

"Oh, sorry. Yes, the rooms are paid for, but to whom should we mail the extra money?"

"We'll send someone for it tomorrow. With proper identification, of course." Jonathon said, feeling very sophisticated.

The cab driver was actually Officer Fullback. "Sorry about that, we thought we'd vetted this place thoroughly."

When they were all in the cab and the suitcases were packed in the trunk, the driver headed back down Wilshire Boulevard. Three blocks later he turned right and drove to an apartment building with a fence around it. A man dressed as a door man rolled the front gate open after the policeman showed identification.

Jonathon wondered if the guy worked for the apartment building owner or was an undercover policeman. There seemed to be a lot of them involved in this. He wished he felt he could trust any of them.

Officer Fullback helped them carry the luggage up to their new five room apartment. "There's food in the kitchen. Help yourselves."

As he went to the front door, Jonathon said, "Excuse me sir, but are we still the Magillacuddys or do we have to change names again."

"We decided there's no point in changing your names, so go back to using your real names," Officer Fullback said. "Oh, and here's a different number for you to call. It's my private number and if anyone else answers hang up and run."

"Is there a problem we don't know about, Officer?" asked Mom.

"Yes Ma'am. We seemed to have sprung a leak in our office."

"A leak?" asked Jonathon, shivers running up his spine yet again. "What do you mean?"

"Somebody in our department is working with this group that's killing people and breaking into your house. We don't know what's going on, but we do have a lead."

"I am supposed to start a new job in the morning," said Richard. "What do I do about that?"

"Yes, we know about that and we think it's a good idea for you to show up for work. Your office knows what's going on and they think maybe you'll be useful in rounding up this gang."

Mom started to protest, but Richard held up his hand. "It'll be fine. Don't worry. And I'll feel better if I can help sort this out."

Jonathon muttered, "Wish I could help." But what could he do? They sure wouldn't let him do undercover police work at his age. Besides, whoever the bad guys were, they seemed to know Jonathon pretty well.

So many questions jumped into his thoughts. *How did the police know so much about their personal lives? Like Richard's new job.* He was even beginning to wonder if that girl he met at the beach—what was her name—might be a spy. Oh yeah, Gloria. She seemed nice enough, but maybe she got huffy because she'd gotten what she was looking for. And learning about Jennifer was just her excuse to make an exit. Plus, maybe she figured whoever was searching the family's stuff had finished by then.

And, he wondered, what was hidden in their house that anybody else would want? War Bonds? He thought Mom said they were in the safety deposit box downtown. But why would anybody want to murder a neighbor over War Bonds? The only thing of value he had was his baseball card collection. But that certainly wasn't worth killing for. Or was it? Did the writing he'd seen on his Babe Ruth card mean something. He thought he remembered thinking it was written in Latin.

Jonathon turned toward the front door when Office Fullback clicked it open. His family was standing by the door staring at him.

"Are you okay, Jonathon?" asked Mom.

"Yeah," said Christopher. "You've been standing there as if you were in another time zone carrying on a conversation."

Jonathon's face heated up, glowing a light red. "Oh, sorry. Just thinking. Didn't realize I was talking out loud." He forced a lopsided smile. "Think I need some sleep." He wasn't sure he trusted anybody anymore, so he decided not to say anything to Officer Fullback. Vaguely, he heard the guy give his real name, but Jonathon was sure he wouldn't remember it. He'd just stick with the nickname.

He nodded and said, "Thanks for your help."

When it was just the family left, Christopher yawned and Mary Anne stretched. Mom checked her watch.

"My heavens," she said, "it almost two a.m. What time do you have to report to work, Richard?"

"Tomorrow I don't have to be there until nine a.m. I have some kind of orientation to go through and paperwork to fill out," he shrugged his shoulders, "After that it's a crap shoot."

In the room designated for the boys', Jonathon picked the bed tucked in a corner and closest to the window. That way anybody coming after him would only have a front-on option of reaching him. When they all used the bathroom and put away their clothes, Jonathon stretched out on his bed and looked out the window.

The morning fog was creeping in, reminding him of Carl Sandburg's poem about fog. The poet had written that the fog crept in on silent cat's paws. Jonathon wasn't a big fan of poetry, but that poem he'd liked. Especially since the family had taken a trip to foggy San Francisco.

He fell asleep listening to his brother Christopher' gentle snoring and Richard's not so gentle snorting.

The room started to shake and the lamp on his bedside table rattled around as if it was going to fall off, but then he saw himself on the same desert land he always was on when this dream occurred. The room wasn't really shaking was it? He couldn't open his eyes to check and he couldn't hear anything rattling or crashing.

In his dream the land was splitting open faster than it usually did. He was running to keep from falling into each chasm as the ground split open beneath him. Just as the last piece of land rumbled and started to crack, he woke up with Christopher standing over him.

"Jonathon! Jonathon! Wake up!" his brother said.

"Wow, buddy," said Richard. "What were you dreaming about?

Jonathon told them his dream and said, "Wish I could say it's okay, but I have that dream a lot and it always scares me silly."

"I don't envy you that," said Christopher.

Richard whispered, "Amen," and headed toward the bathroom, toothbrush in hand.

Jonathon didn't tell his brothers how much that dream troubled him and how each time it occurred was worse. He started having the dream when Dad had gone off on his last overseas mission, in May of 1941. He'd been stationed in the Philippines on the island of Bataan and they hadn't heard from him often since Japan bombed Pearl Harbor on December 7th, 1941.

More than a year since he'd left home and Jonathon noticed that Mom hadn't had any news from him since the letter in August. And that was postmarked in June.

"Jonathon," said Christopher. "Are you alright? Ever since Dr. Ringwaldt was murdered you've seemed distracted."

"Aren't you? Doesn't it seemed strange that people on our street are dying?"

Christopher raised his eyebrows. "Yes, but what can we do about it?"

"I don't know, but I can't just hide and watch from a distance," said Jonathon. "I've got to do something." He reached for his watch. "It's 7 o'clock, is anybody else up?"

"Richard's still in the bathroom, but I thought I heard somebody in the kitchen," said Christopher.

"Probably Mom. Not like Mary Anne to get up this early unless she has to," said Jonathon. He rolled toward the wall and curled into a fetal position. "Think I'm going to try for some more shuteye."

"I'm hungry," said Christopher, slipping on the clothes he'd worn the night before. "Sleep well and no more bad dreams."

Jonathon didn't even hear his brother leave the room. But an hour later he heard Richard opening and shutting dresser drawers and muttering about not finding anything. Where had he put his ties?

"You must be excited about having a job, brother mine. And one that might make a difference." Jonathon slapped Richard lightly on the shoulder. A male hug. Only girls gave real hugs.

Well, unless the guy was putting a move on his girlfriend. He remembered how it felt when he held Jennifer close. Stirred his body up, he knew. He wondered what it felt like for a girl to be hugged by a guy. Jennifer always seemed to step closer. Even thinking about that made Jonathon's body perk up.

"Gotta go," said Richard with an extra bit of excitement in his voice. "Wish me luck."

"I'm proud of you, Richard," Jonathon said. "Wish I could go with you."

"You've got to stay and protect our family," Richard squeezed his brother's arm. "You're the sane one. The rest of us have a screw loose."

Chapter 21

"D ON'T KNOW ABOUT THAT," whispered Jonathon. "Stay safe and let us know what's happening in the real world," he added louder.

After Jonathon was done in the bathroom, beating Mary Anne into the room thanks to his size twelve feet, he wandered into the kitchen where Mom was rearranging the cookware to her liking. He grabbed a banana and juice, which he munched down while four pieces of bread were toasting. When the toast was nicely smeared with honey, Jonathon held the slices in a paper napkin and wandered into the living/dining room area. He sat at the dining table facing the rear window.

Oh, there's a balcony outside the sliding glass door. And, he noticed, there were chairs out there, one of which was occupied by Christopher, who seemed to be mesmerized by something on the ground five stories down.

When he joined his brother, Jonathon looked to see what was so fascinating on the ground. Three young women were down by a swimming pool, dressed in swimming suits and lying on chaise lounges sunning themselves, two blondes and a brunette. The blondes were busty and a bit on the skinny side for Jonathon's taste, but the brunette was a stunner. She filled out her suit with enough breast to squeeze together above the suit, but she didn't look like she was going to pop out of the garment. Her legs were long and sleek. No high-heeled shoes for that baby. She looked like she could be a long-distance runner and even from five stories up, he could see she was well muscled.

She made him miss Jennifer so much he could taste it.

Christopher seemed to be focusing on the smaller of the two blondes who got off her chair, stretched and slipped into the pool. She took off toward the deep end of the pool with a strong steady stroke, did a flip when she got there and headed back to the shallow end.

"Man, "said Christopher, "I'd be happy to swim with her any day of the week."

"Go down and join her," said Jonathon. "What else are you going to do all day?"

"Got to do my school work first. That big policeman…"

"You mean the one built like a fullback? That's what I call him."

"The one who drove us here last night?"

Jonathon nodded.

"Anyway, Officer Fullback brought us more school work. There's some for you too."

"I'll do it later. I've got to get some exercise first or I'll go crazy."

Jonathon stood and scanned the back yard. It was all fenced in, but there was a gate in the right-hand corner. He looked up and over the stockade fence trying to see where the building was in relationship to their house. At first, he didn't recognize any of the buildings, but then caught a glimpse of what he thought was the Wilshire Boulevard Department store where Granny always took them for their school clothes. *No, that couldn't be the store, because he was looking out the back of the building.* He decided he'd just have to sneak out and figure out where he was when he got to the front of the building. Then he remembered that Granny didn't have a place to stay. Would she show up at their house and wonder where they were?

"What's Granny going to do now that her lease is up?" Jonathon turned toward Christopher, who turned his palms up and shook his head.

"Mom doesn't know and she's worried."

"Didn't she ask Officer Fullback?"

Christopher nodded, "He didn't know. Said he looked into it."

Jonathon's back muscles tensed up. "This isn't good. We can't live our lives like this."

"What can we do about it?"

"I don't know," said Jonathon, "but I'm going to find out." He looked over the fence again and pointed. "Do you see any buildings you recognize?"

Christopher came to the balcony edge and looked where his brother was pointing. He shook his head. "No."

"Our apartment is at the back of this building, so if I go around to the front and turn left I'll get to Van Ness and our house."

"Okay? Then what?"

"Don't tell Mom and Mary Anne, but I'm going to go see what's going on."

Christopher grabbed Jonathon's arm. "Don't do that! You could get yourself hurt or killed."

"I can't just sit here and wait."

"How're you gonna get past Mom?"

"Just tell her I'm getting some exercise. I'll wear my bathing suit under my jeans."

"You tell her that yourself. I think you're just asking for trouble."

"Don't worry. I'll be fine."

"It's your hide, brother. Just be careful and you'd better be back by lunch time."

"Won't make lunch. If she asks, tell Mom I'll be back by three thirty."

Jonathon put on his swim suit under his crisp blue jeans, rolled the cuffs, exposing white socks, and laced up his high-top Keds. He could sneak around in them very easily. He put on a clean tee shirt and headed toward the front door.

Mary Anne looked up from the homework she was doing at the dining area table. She opened mouth to speak, but Jonathon put a finger to his lips and shook his head.

He pointed toward Mom, who was sleeping in a chair on the other side of the room. He mouthed that he was just going out for some air.

Mary Anne nodded and looked back at her book.

First hurdle leapt, he thought, as he slipped out the door, making sure not to let it click shut. He tested it to see if it was fully closed.

Instead of taking the elevator, he went down the set of stairs that headed toward the back of the building, hoping it would take him down to the basement and the pool area. But when he got to the sign for the pool, he noticed the stairs went down at least one more flight.

A sub-basement. He wondered if it was below the ground level. And if it was, would there be an outside set of stairs leading to ground level. *Worth a shot,* he thought. It was dark down those stairs and he couldn't see how low they went. Running his hand along the wall in part to feel his way and in part to stabilize himself, Jonathon headed down the steps.

He heard a drip, drip noise coming from below him and felt the dampness increase as he moved downward. He wondered if there were leaky pipes and if so, were they sewer pipes. He wasn't too keen in getting caught in dirty water. Oh well, he thought, remembering what Granddaddy used to say, "In for a penny, in for a pound."

When he was little, he wondered what that meant. Shouldn't it be a dollar? But Granddaddy explained it was a British saying and a pound was the English version of a dollar.

He stopped to let his eyes adjust to the almost pitch-black darkness around him. There had to be a light switch somewhere, but he didn't want to find it. He didn't want any light in case a janitor looked down there. Besides, how would he turn it off after he was out of the building? Provided he could find a door that led out of the building. Then he realized there was some light coming from the end of what seemed to be a short hallway.

The janitor's office? But who would want an office down here? Maybe it was daylight showing through a crack in a doorway?

His left foot connected with more cement, but he couldn't feel the edge of a step. He brought his right foot next its mate and realized he was on solid ground. Still running his hand along the now damp wall, he edged toward the light. Three steps later the toe of his right shoe collided with metal. He reached his hand out and felt along what might be a door.

He slid his hand down until he felt the doorknob. But the knob wouldn't rotate under his pressure. Of course, the door was locked, but was there a key hidden close by? He felt back up the door until he came to the top. The head jamb was deep enough to hold a key, so Jonathon slid his hand along until he felt the key.

In a minute, the door was open and light came streaming in. Now what should he do with the key? There appeared to be enough room at the bottom to slip the key under after he'd locked the door from the outside. But to be on the safe side, once he was out, he shut the door and holding it firmly closed with one hand, he reached down and slipped the key under.

Yes! His plan would work. After retrieving the key, then securely locking the door and reinserting the key under the door, he ran up the outside steps. Hoping the janitor would just think the key had fallen off the ledge during the last earthquake, he congratulated himself. *Second hurdle leapt.*

When he got to the top step, he realized he'd come out clear of the fenced-in pool area, but there was still a chain-link barrier around the entire property. Could he just climb it without anybody spotting him?

He looked around the corner of the building toward what he thought must be the front entrance, but it turned out the building wasn't square. The front was another turn away.

Things were definitely going his way. If he climbed the fence here, he'd be least likely to be seen. Still, there was a steep drop just on the other side of the fence with a small stream at the bottom. Well it would be a stream when winter rains came. Now it was just a ditch. He'd have to climb down the outside of the fence, he couldn't just jump from the top.

Safely down, Jonathon steadied himself by hanging on to the fence. He oriented himself to what was around him and how exposed he would be as he made his way toward the front of the building. Live oaks were growing up out of the ravine, so his cover was good there. He figured anybody looking out the windows in the neighboring building wouldn't be able to see him, but what about anybody looking out the end apartment in his building? Maybe the angle would be too steep and anybody looking out wouldn't be able to look straight down. He'd just have to trust that was the case, hoping the occupants were gone to work for the day.

He hoped he'd know which building was his when he wanted to get back in. But he stopped in his tracks when he realized he hadn't made a plan as to how he was going to get back in. Well, he'd worry about that later. He inched his way along the fence until he came to the corner of the fence and breathed a sigh of relief when the ravine slowly leveled off, giving him enough room to move freely. Soon after that, he came to an alleyway that lead to an intersecting street.

He looked up to see if he could see the Wilshire Department store roof so he could use that as a direction focus. And luck was still with him. Right in front of him was the Wilton Place elementary school he'd gone to years ago during Dad's last deployment. He knew exactly where he was. He looked around to see if anybody saw him emerge onto the street.

There was a man walking toward him, but he paid Jonathon no mind as he shuffled along muttering to himself.

Jonathon walked by him with his head down and headed down the street to Wilshire Boulevard. When he got to the intersection, he debated whether he should walk down the Boulevard or just stay on the street he was on until he got to the street Eddie lived on.

Either way, he ran the risk of seeing somebody he knew. His friends were in school he figured and their moms were at work or volunteering, so the chances were small. Most of the fathers were off fighting the war.

He continued down the street he was on, but two blocks later he regretted his choice. There was Old Lady Fontaine, sweeping her front porch and scanning the street for any gossip she could pick up. And she was good at making up stories to spread.

Jonathon slipped behind a telephone pole and turned sideways when she moved to his side of her steps. Everybody knew she had weak eyes, making it easier for him to evade her. When Mrs. Fontaine looked down to keep from stumbling as she moved to the next lower stair down, Jonathon stepped from behind the pole and hurried into the alleyway two houses up.

He caught a glimpse of the old lady looking in his direction, but he was sure he was moving fast enough to only be a blur to her. In any case, he figured he was safe.

He decided to just stay in the alleyway until he got to Van Ness Avenue. Less likely to be seen, except by a maid or repair man who wouldn't recognize him. Dodging garbage cans and light poles and the occasional car, Jonathon sprinted down to his street and turned right toward his house. But three doors up from his house, he skidded to a halt and ducked down behind lamppost with a raised base. There were three unmarked police cars with flashing lights in front of his house and more patrol cars parked in front of Dr. Ringwaldt's house. Two more cars were parked in the dead man's driveway.

A big man came out their neighbor's house and Jonathon sucked in his breath. "Dad?" he whispered. "That looks like Dad," he said softly. "What would he be doing here?"

Chapter 22

H E WAS HALF WAY down the street before he realized it probably was not his father. After all, his father was in the Pacific Ocean somewhere. And what would he have to do with a crime scene? He was a Marine, not a policeman or in the OSS. Still, just to be safe, Jonathon looked at the ground to hide his face and sauntered across the street.

Two houses down, he turned to look back toward his house. Why were the police carrying boxes out? What did they find that had anything to do with this mystery? It took all his willpower to not run back across the Avenue and grab the boxes away, demanding them to leave his family alone! His body shook with anger. *What? His baseball card collection had secret information written on it? Rather than talking about Lou Gehrig's life and career, the card had code on how to save the Third Reich? That's ridiculous.*

He sat on the curb, not even caring if the policemen saw him. What would they do to him, anyway? In his anger and confusion, he grabbed fistfuls of grass and pulled them up by the roots.

The action calmed him some, but when he looked down, he realized he'd made a sizable bald patch beside him. Oh great, he'd better not let Mr. Hermann see who'd done that. He liked his lawn to be perfect and he'd never completely forgiven Mary Anne for picking the newly-opened orchid flower blooming for the first time in a hundred years. The man was in tears when he told Mom about it. Mary Anne wasn't allowed to play outside of the yard for weeks.

"But it was so pretty," she'd said.

Jonathon got up, dusted off his jeans, and shook grass leaves out of the rolled-up cuffs. His rubbed his dirty fingers along his thighs and picked dirt out from under his nails. There wasn't a thing he could do with all those officials wandering around. They wouldn't let him in his house, that was for sure.

He wandered further down his block until he came to the next alleyway and turned left. He figured he'd go two more blocks and turn left again. That way he could get back to Wilshire Boulevard and back to their apartment.

As he walked, he got the sense that someone was following him. He started to run and still felt someone else was there, but when he stopped and looked behind him, the alley was empty. Strange, he thought. Movement behind him near a fence caught his eye. Was it a person?

He sighed in relief. Just a grey tabby cat, with its tail standing straight up, looking very proud of itself.

Jonathon decided he was just having a case of the willies and turned forward to continue his way down to the next cross street. Maybe he'd had enough for the day. He'd just go back to his family.

He looked at his watch and, when he saw it was almost one o'clock, he realized his stomach was growling. He was thirsty as well.

But when he turned left at the next street, a grey Studebaker was parked at the curb and Mr. Jungen stood in front of Jonathon, trying to block his way.

Another man, a big man—so big he made Jonathon feel small—grabbed Jonathon by the arm and pulled him toward the car. Looked like the guy from the tobacco shop from last night.

Jonathon twisted in the man's arms and tried to kick backward into his shins, but the man picked him up as if he were made of paper. The man got in to the car and dragged Jonathon in behind him.

"Calm down, Jonathon," said Mr. Jungen, as he got behind the steering wheel. "We mean you no harm."

"Sure you don't, that's why you attacked me and shoved me into this car." Jonathon pulled with all his might against the man holding him, but the fellow just growled at him and tighten his grip.

"Let go of me, you goon."

"Zis will not do, Jonathon," said the big ape.

Mr. Jungen moved out into traffic. "We're just trying to keep you safe."

"By abducting me? How does that keep me safe?"

"*Ve* are not abducting you, *kinder. Ve* are taking *zu* to your *vater.*"

"My what?"

"We're taking you to your father. He saw you at your house." Mr. Jungen pulled away from the curb.

"Dad's somewhere in the Pacific Ocean killing Japs." Jonathon snarled. "Stop lying to me."

Mr. Jungen stopped his car at a stop sign and Jonathon opened the door on his side. He jumped out just as another car pulled up beside him, barely giving him room to avoid being hit. He dodged behind that car ignoring the yells from Mr. Jungen and the goon who was trying to get out of the car through the door Jonathon had left open.

But luck was with Jonathon and a big black Cadillac like the ones the gangsters in the movies always drove pulled up behind. The driver honked his horn at Mr. Jungen and edged toward his bumper. As the Studebaker drove forward, Jonathon ducked into an alleyway and hid behind an oversized garbage can.

He counted to fifty, peeked out from the behind the can, and, seeing the coast was clear, ran away from Wilshire Boulevard. He ran for three blocks and turned right on the cross avenue. He angled toward the apartment building.

Finally, he saw he was a block from the building he now called home. But he was a block above where he needed to be, so he crossed the street and was about to turn left, when somebody yelled, "Hey, Jonathon!"

Chapter 23

HE TURNED TOWARD THE voice and there was Richard. He stopped and waited for his brother to catch up to him. "What are you doing here? I thought you were at work today."

Richard nodded. "I was, but they were finished with their training session and said I could go home." He stared into Jonathon's eyes and held onto his arm. "They also said to make sure you were alright and to stay put in the apartment."

"Umm," said Jonathon, but Richard held his hand up.

"What did they mean? And why are you outside the compound?"

"How did they know I had gotten out? And why do they care?"

"That's what they do. And they want to keep you safe."

"Who are these people? Are these the people you work for?"

Richard nodded. "I can't tell you anything more than they're on our side. You've gotta trust me on this." He turned Jonathon around and they headed toward the front gate. "You do realize you've scared Mom half to death. She thought you'd been kidnapped."

"I was. Briefly."

"Okay," said Richard, raising his eyebrows. He nodded at the guard who opened the front gate for them and steered Jonathon to a bench at the side of the building along the edge of a nice garden planted for the residents. Richard said, "Spill, brother mine."

Jonathon told his brother about his day and Richard took notes, including one that said "secure subbasement door at top."

"And one of the guys coming out of Dr. Ringwaldt's house looked just like Dad."

"Really?"

"Yeah, but it couldn't have been." Jonathon looked into his brother's eyes, but Richard dropped eye contact. "Could it?"

"Probably not. When did you get abducted?"

"When I was on my way back here."

"What happened?"

As Jonathon told his story, Richard's eyes narrowed and he filled two more pages in his notebook.

"Don't tell Mom or the twins about this, Jonathon. And do not ever go out like that again."

"You're not in charge here, Richard. I can't just stay here and be helpless."

"It's too dangerous for you to be out here."

"Why is it more dangerous for me to be out there than it is for you? What makes you so special?"

"Because I'm being trained to handle situations like this."

"Can't you arrange for me to do something? I've got to help."

Richard opened the front door of their building and nodded for Jonathon to go in first. They both scanned the foyer to see if anybody suspicious was lurking there.

But what did suspicious look like? There was an elderly woman, probably close to sixty, sitting in a chair looking out the window. Dressed to go someplace nice.

Quite the picture of peaches and cream, was this woman, thought Jonathon. Wouldn't hurt a fly. But is that what she wanted them to think? Did she actually have a pistol hidden in her handbag? She didn't appear to sinister. She reminded him of Granny. Not somebody to mess with, but definitely a heart of gold.

Still, she had nodded at them when they came in the door and then went back to looking out the window. She was probably just waiting for a ride.

Jonathon saw a partitioned off section of the lobby partially hiding what looked like mailboxes. He nodded in that direction and asked Richard. "Do you think we have a mail box?"

Richard looked puzzled and spread his hand palms up. "Don't know. Hadn't even thought about it."

They walked over to see if they could figure out how they could tell if one was theirs. But who would send them mail here? Nothing obvious popped out at them.

Jonathon waved his hands, as if to shoo away that worry and said, "Let's just go up and let me get my lecture over with."

Chapter 24

BUT WHEN THEY GOT to their new home, Mom was reading in the living room and the twins were playing a game of Gin Rummy. She looked up and glowered at Jonathon. "Glad you made it back in one piece."

"You're not angry with me?" Jonathon asked, with shock registering on his face.

"Of course I'm angry. I'm banning you from stepping out of this apartment for a week."

"Do you mean the apartment itself or the building?"

"The apartment."

"I can't even go to the swimming pool?"

"That is correct."

"Aw Mom. What'll I do for a whole week?"

"Work on your Latin homework. You're slipping there."

Jonathon thought maybe it would be a good idea to change the subject. "I keep meaning to ask what Granny's going to do now? Is she coming to stay with us here?"

"Granny's fine. She's on the train to visit friends in New York and then she's going down to Annapolis for your grandfather's funeral."

Mary Anne's face sagged. "I guess I can't go, huh?"

"I'm sorry dear, but I don't think it's wise. I don't want you riding the train by yourself, especially with all these suspicious people stalking us."

Jonathon opened his mouth to ask another question, but Mom raised her hand and shook her head. "I am so angry with you right now, I want you to go to your room until dinner time."

She turned to Christopher and Mary Anne. "It's time for you to finish your school work and then you may go to the pool. But if there's anybody else there, I want you to come right back up here. Whoever these people are, they're deadly serious."

"Yes Ma'am," said Mary Anne, moving back to the dining table, which was half full of books and paper from her notebook.

"I just have a couple chapters in my history book to read. May I just read here?" Christopher asked.

"As long as you actually read. Don't you have to write notes?"

"I've got my notebook and a pencil with me."

She turned back toward Jonathon and said, "I thought I told you to go to your room." She looked at Richard, who'd been standing near the front door looking as if he might just leave again.

Jonathon walked down the hall toward his bedroom, but turned at the kitchen. "May I get something to eat first?"

Mom nodded and asked Richard, "How was your first day at work? Did you learn a lot?"

"Boy did I! Now I can see why Dad gets so excited about what he's doing."

"Oh? Do you know what he's doing?"

Richard paused and his face flushed a little pink to his cheeks. "No, but he's always seemed so excited to go to work each day. That's what I mean."

"I see. Like I feel when I go to my job at Lockheed?"

Richard nodded. "I guess so."

Jonathon came back out of the kitchen and Richard looked in his direction, nodding his head toward their bedroom.

"I'm a little tired from learning all this stuff, Mom. If you don't mind, I'm going to take a rest. I've got some more reading to do," Richard said.

"That's fine. Dinner will be at six."

When they were in their bedroom, Jonathon patted his bed for Richard to come sit there. "I did tell you I thought I saw Dad today, didn't I?"

Richard nodded. "Yeah, but you must have been mistaken. Why wouldn't we have heard from him?"

"How would I know? But don't you remember those Marines coming to the house last week? Just after we heard about Granddaddy?"

"What of it?"

"Maybe he's here on a secret mission? Maybe he's here to see if there's a counteragent in the service?"

"Come on. Dad's in the navy. He's not a spy." Richard snorted and frowned at his brother.

"Do we really know that? I mean sure he's in the navy, but maybe he's been recruited to do spy work during the war?"

"But if he's been in the Pacific Theatre all this time, why would he suddenly be investigating a Nazi spy ring?" Richard shook his head. "I think this is farfetched."

Jonathon reached for his Latin book and slumped back on his bed. "I guess you're right." He opened the book as Richard stood up. "But that guy sure looked like him."

"Well, they say everyone has a *doppelganger.*"

"A what?"

"You know, someone who looks exactly like you."

Jonathon scrunched up his mouth and muttered, "Maybe." He opened his book to his assignment and translated a passage that in English read, "all Gaul is divided into three parts..." Oh yeah, Julius Caesar, another dictator's conquering words.

He wondered if the world was meant to be ruled by dictators. Most of them seemed to be egomaniacal bullies. This war had three such leaders. Hitler who wanted to make the world pure for his Master Race. Mussolini who wanted who knew what? And Emperor Hirohito, who just wanted more land it seemed and probably more power. That's probably what they all wanted. In any case, Jonathon felt the Allied Forces needed to defeat them all.

He finished about two thirds of the translation before he fell asleep. This time his dream seemed to be in another place. Not California. Though how he knew it was different was beyond him, since all he ever saw was desert. Maybe the desert looked different. Didn't matter, he still woke up in a sweat and a parched feeling in his mouth.

He needed a breath of fresh air. He looked over at Richard's bed, but his brother was lying on his back sound asleep, his lips puffing in and out with every breath.

Jonathon tiptoed out of the room, poured himself a glass of water and slid open the sliding door to the balcony. Mom was sitting there knitting a shawl for a wounded soldier and watching the twins bounce around in the pool below her.

"May I sit out here for a little bit, Mom?" When she nodded, he pulled up another chair and sat beside her, raising his feet to the railing.

"I'm sorry about today."

"I hope so."

"It's just I can't wait around hoping somebody will rescue us. That's not who I am."

"Is that why you keep having your earthquake dream?"

"You know about that dream?"

"We all do, dear."

"Oh."

Mom reached over and patted Jonathon's arm. "Your dad says he used to have a similar kind of dream, except his involved sitting in a huge oak tree that was being cut down. He couldn't get the lumberjack to hear him and he couldn't get down."

"I feel so powerless."

"I know. So do I."

Jonathon looked at Mom, his eyes widening and his mouth dropping open. "You? You always look like you're in control."

"I'm the grown-up. I'm supposed to be in control. I'm supposed to protect us, since your dad isn't here to do that."

"Do you know where Dad is?"

Mom shook her head and wiped away a tear that was trickling down her cheek.

"I thought I saw him today."

Mom's eyebrows almost disappeared into her hair line. "Where? When?"

Jonathon told her where he'd gone and what he'd seen. "It couldn't have been Dad, though? He's not here?"

Mom sighed. "Last I heard he was still fighting the Japanese."

"Didn't you say you thought he'd called and used his secret signal?"

"Well, I did have that strange phone call last week." Mom stopped and tilted her head. "But whoever whispered into the phone didn't sound like your dad."

Chapter 25

"**W**HAT DO YOU MEAN?"

"Well, Dad's voice is deeper than yours. He sings bass." Mom smiled. "I miss hearing him sing."

"So, what did this voice sound like?"

"Almost falsetto. Could have been a woman's voice."

Jonathon pinched his vocal chords and squeaked out, "You mean like this?"

Mom squinched her eyes shut, nodded and shuddered. "I am not a big fan of falsetto," she said.

Jonathon stood up and stretched.

Down below him, Mary Anne. and Christopher were drying off. Christopher flicked his towel at his sister who squealed and skipped out of reach.

Before he slid the door open, Jonathon stopped and looked down at his mother. "Mom? Aren't you going stir crazy?"

She shook her head. "Not really. It's kind of like a vacation for me."

"Yeah," he stopped and started again, "Yes, but don't you want to solve this mystery?"

"How can I? Where would I start? No, I think I'll leave that to the police."

"I feel like I'm trapped in a cage," said Jonathon.

"I know, honey, and I'm sorry, but there's nothing we can do about it."

Jonathon jerked the sliding door back and stepped into the living room. "There's gotta be something I can do," he muttered and slid the door closed with a solid click.

Richard was sitting by the dining area in an overstuffed chair. He looked at his brother and asked. "Are you feeling better?"

"No. I can't stay in here doing nothing. And for how long? I need to go for a run."

"I understand, but I'm afraid you're stuck."

"At least you've got a job to go to." Jonathon grabbed a glass of water from the kitchen and stomped back to his part of the bedroom, sloshing water left and right.

Just as Jonathon pulled out his Latin book again, Christopher came into the room. "You should have come swimming with us, Jonathon. The water was great!"

"Could I have swum from there to the ocean?" Jonathon snarled.

Christopher's mouth dropped open. "What did I do?"

Jonathon looked back at his book and grabbed his notebook. But try as he might, his mind kept wandering to his baseball card collection and why he thought he'd seen a detective carrying the box he stored them in out of the house.

"Wait a minute!" he shouted, dropping his books and jerking open the door to his room. He ran up the hall yelling, "Mom! Richard!"

Mary Anne popped out of her room. Mom and Richard came in from the balcony. And Christopher yelled from the bathroom, "I'll be out in a minute."

Jonathon jittered from foot to foot. "Do you remember, Richard, I told you about those men taking my baseball card collection? I think I've figured out what they were looking for."

"What's that?" asked Richard.

"Couple of years ago, Dr. Ringwaldt gave me a Babe Ruth card in perfect condition except for this strange writing on the bottom."

"What did the writing say?" Asked Mom.

"Well, that's the thing. The writing was so small, I couldn't read it. And when I used my magnifying glass, I couldn't understand the words."

"Okay? So what's the big deal?" asked Mary Anne.

A dripping wet Christopher, with a towel wrapped around his waist, was standing in the bathroom doorway. "You mean the card that mentions Ruth's 400th homerun?"

Jonathon nodded. "I've figured it out! It was a code written in Latin!"

Mom cocked her head to the side.

Richard shook his head. "So? Maybe he just wanted you to study Latin in school and thought this would motivate you."

Mary Anne nodded, "You were his favorite. He thought you could really go places you're so smart."

"Thank you, but I think he wanted me to hide a secret for him."

"Why would he risk putting you in danger?" asked Mom.

"The card was printed in 1936, the year after Ruth retired, but Dr. Ringwaldt didn't give it to me until 1940. He probably didn't think he was putting me in danger."

"Okay, so why give the code to you?" asked Richard.

"Safe keeping, I guess."

"Seems farfetched to me," said Christopher shutting the bathroom door. "But maybe you should call the police about it!" he shouted through the door.

"If I'm so smart, how come nobody in this family ever thinks my ideas are any good?" asked Jonathon, slumping into a chair.

"It's not that honey." Mom came over to pat Jonathon on his shoulder.

He jerked away. Comfort was not what he wanted. Answers were what he wanted. "Well, may I at least call Jack and tell him what I'm thinking?"

"Why don't I tell my boss tomorrow?"

"What good will that do?" asked Jonathon.

"He's got the right connections. He'll know whom to call."

"Thanks, but I don't suppose you could call now?"

Richard shook his head. "This is not a secure line."

"Okay." Jonathon turned toward Mom, figuring he should change the subject. "When's dinner?"

"I'm just about to start it."

"Want some help?"

"Mary Anne's going to help. She's got a new recipe she wants to try."

Jonathon slouched back to his room. Maybe he could try to remember what Dr. Ringwaltdt's message was. The Latin version. He sat on his bed and closed his eyes, trying to visualize the card.

The front was a picture of Ruth with his arm propped up on a fence and his body turned three-quarters the way toward to viewer, as if they were having a neighborly conversation. His signature and basic information were below the picture, but somebody had printed in black ink below the signature.

Jonathon's head nodded toward his chest and he dropped the pencil he was holding. The next thing he knew he was standing to the right of third base keeping his eye on the batter's stance. The batter swung and grounded the ball right toward Jonathon, but just as it reached him the ground rumbled and cracks appeared. He dove to grab the ball before it plummeted into the chasm before him. He reached forward, stretching his arm and torso as far as he could, but the ball teetered on the edge of the void. Jonathon tried to elongate his body just a bit more, digging in with his toes to keep from disappearing over the edge. The ball tipped the edge of his glove before careening into the abyss.

He woke up when his head bumped onto the floor beside his bed. He pushed his body back up onto his bed and curled into a ball until he stopped shaking.

Chapter 26

"WHAT WERE YOU DREAMING about this time?" Christopher asked looking down at his brother, his eyes bright with worry.

"Baseball and earthquakes," said Jonathon, rubbing his hand across his forehead. "I've gotta get some exercise. I'm going nuts with nothing do to."

"Do you think that's why you're having your earthquake nightmare so frequently?"

"Maybe."

"You didn't start to have these dreams until Dad went away, right?"

"Yeah, I guess that's when they started."

"He'll be alright." Christopher smiled. "Anyway, Mom asked me to tell you dinner's ready."

When the family was seated, Mary Anne walked in carrying a big tureen full of something steamy hot. She approached the table looking down at the bowl and walking heel to toe.

Jonathon released his breath when she placed the container by Mom. And he smiled when he heard the sigh of exhaled air come from the rest of his family.

"Well done, Sis," said her twin.

Mary Anne grinned as she sat at her place. "Didn't spill a drop!"

After saying grace, Mom ladle out big bowls of soup which wafted up the aroma of thyme, rosemary and garlic. When everyone was served, she dipped her soup spoon toward the back of her bowl and scooped up a spoonful of carrots, potatoes and celery.

No meat, Jonathon noticed, but the broth was so rich, he hardly missed it. And there were crusty chunks of rye bread to make the whole meal very filling. He asked for seconds when everybody's bowl was empty.

Mary Anne's smile lit up the room when she realized the tureen had hardly a drop left in it at the end of the meal.

Christopher patted his stomach. "Good meal, Mary Anne. I'm happy."

"I'm proud of you, sweetheart," said Mom. "Where'd you find the recipe?"

"Well, I found a meat version of it in *Fanny Farmer*, but I made up which herbs and spices to add to make it seem heartier."

"You'll make someone a good wife someday." Richard smiled and laid his napkin by his place.

"Thank you," said Mary Anne. "But not before I become a famous chef."

"Girls can't be chefs," said Christopher, "that's a man's job."

"We'll see about that," said Mom and Mary Anne together.

Everybody laughed, but Mom said "They all said a woman couldn't be a tool and dye designer, but look at me."

"Yes, but that's because of the war," said Jonathon.

"What difference should that make?" Mary Anne put her hands on her hips and frowned.

"Men will need their jobs back when the war is over," said Christopher.

Richard nodded, "And women should be back to the making a home and a family."

"Maybe women can do both," said Mom. "Now who's turn is it to do the dishes?"

"I'll do them," said Jonathon, "give me something to do."

"I'll help you clear the table, Jonathon," said Christopher.

While he was washing the dishes, Jonathon thought about his trip to their house earlier in the day. He remembered seeing the men coming out of his house carrying several boxes each. Where did all those boxes come from? Was his whole family secretly storing stuff having to do with this war?

If so, what? And why? And did Mom know they were storing secrets?

He thought back to the Babe Ruth baseball card. Why had Dr. Ringwaldt given Jonathon the card? And why had he deliberately decreased its trading value by defacing it with extra words? And what was Jonathon supposed to do with it?

He wished he could talk to Jennifer, if she would ever talk to him again. How long did he have to be away before she'd start dating somebody else? Kurt sure wanted to date her. After all, she was the best girl in school, not just in the looks department but also the brains.

What would she think of what he'd been through? And in reality, what had he'd been through? Yeah, finding your neighbor stabbed to death wasn't all that nice, but at least he, Jonathon, hadn't been murdered or even really hurt. If he had to admit it, the guy who pushed him into Mr. Jungen's car hadn't hurt him.

Made him mad, yes. Hurt him, no.

And not going to school every day had its upside. At least he didn't have to deal with teachers wanting their homework on time.

Still, he missed talking with his friends and he missed the discussions he had in history class. Doctor Gordon was a cool guy. He was good at telling stories that turned out to be history lessons. And he liked his students to question what he said.

Mostly though, what Jonathon missed was being able to move around and not hole up in a dumb apartment building.

Tomorrow he'd ask Mom if she'd let him at least go swimming. But now he'd do more in his Latin book. Maybe improve his grade in that class. He gathered up his book, notebook and several pencils and headed back to the living room.

The twins had already commandeered the dining room table and Richard was sprawled out on the sofa reading, listening to the radio. Doris Day was crooning "Invitation to the Blues and the Les Brown's Band of Renown was backing her up. She had a good voice and was very perky, but Jonathon liked Ella Fitzgerald's sultry voice better.

He sat on the floor beside the coffee table and spread out his stuff. He finished translating the bit about all Gaul being divided into three parts. He tried to visualize what three parts were meant. He thought Gaul was just Italy, but this made it seem as if France, Germany, England and at least parts of Africa were included. Proving once again that there had always been land grabbing rulers who wanted to own it all.

After he finished writing down his translation and double checking the words he wasn't sure of, he tried visualizing what was written on his baseball card. What a minute! He remembered part of what was written translated "All of Germany encompasses," what? What did it encompass? Europe? The Eastern Hemisphere? Was it a plan to conquer all of that? But what was the warning? His mind was reeling. What did any of this have to do with anything? He decided to try to let it all go rather than give himself a headache.

"Does anybody mind if I change the station and listen to "Inner Sanctum?"

"Good idea," said Mary Anne.

"I'm going to bed," said Mom. "And I want the rest of you in bed at the end of the program."

"Yes ma'am and good night," Jonathon and his siblings all answered.

The program started with its usual creaky door and the announcer's deep voice saying "Welcome to The Inner Sanctum."

Mary Anne giggled and shuddered. "I love that opening."

Richard nodded, "Sends a shiver up my spine every time."

The story of a murder, and the mystery surrounding it, made Jonathon feel like the world was conspiring to keep him in suspense, but he let the story unfold and take him to a different place. As if his problems could be solved in half an hour.

Christopher figured out who the villain was fifteen minutes into the story, but nobody else thought he was right.

"But he wasn't in the building when the shots were fired," protested Richard.

"And he's such a nice guy," added Mary Anne.

Christopher stood up and stretched, keeping his grin glowing when he was proven right.

"Good night," said Mary Anne. "I get first dibs on the bathroom."

"Well, just don't take all night," grumbled Jonathon.

Fifteen minutes later the boys were allowed in to brush their teeth and get ready for bed.

When they'd settled into their beds, Jonathon turned to Richard. "You are going to work tomorrow, right?"

Richard nodded as he yawned. "I'm supposed to be there at seven."

"That early?" asked Christopher.

"Yep."

"This is going to sound farfetched, but ask them to check the Latin on my 1936 Babe Ruth baseball card." Jonathon rolled onto his side so he was facing his brothers.

"Why would they have your cards? I know there are the world to you, but still, what do they have to do with anything?" Christopher asked.

"I don't know," said Jonathon with a shake of his head. "But I saw them carry the box out of our house today."

"Wait, you went to our house today?"

Jonathon nodded.

"Boy, are you in a heap of trouble." Christopher shook his head.

"I know. But I feel so trapped waiting in this apartment."

"I, for one, need some sleep," said Richard, turning the overhead light off.

Jonathon rolled onto his back and Christopher curled up into his usual fetal position. "Goodnight," they said in unison.

Chapter 27

JONATHON'S MIND KEPT SPINNING. What if the Germans were to infiltrate the U.S. government? What if Nazis were secretly taking over the East coast and the Japs were taking over the West already?

He rubbed his forehead and stared up at the ceiling. He grabbed the novel he was reading for English, *For Whom the Bell Tolls*. A depressing story if he'd ever read one. But he might as well finish it.

He fell asleep during the love scene between Pillar and Robert Jordan. *He dreamt that he and Jennifer were in the mountains and it was raining. In the distance they could hear booming and thought it was thunder, but then Jonathon realized the booms were coming too frequently to be thunder.*

Guns? Were people shooting off cannons nearby? The ground was shaking with each boom, but it didn't feel like an earthquake. He'd heard cannon fire at the various bases where they'd been stationed, so he was sure that's what he was feeling.

Then he heard voices shouting things like "Take cover! We're being attacked! He pulled Jennifer close and curled around her. He spotted a large cave above them. He touched Jennifer's shoulder and pointed up. She nodded and they ran toward the cave. Just as they reached the entrance, something whistled overhead and exploded beside them, sending shards of rock flying everywhere.

Jennifer screamed and grabbed her leg. Blood spurted between her fingers. He couldn't stop the bleeding. His girlfriend was dying and there wasn't a thing he could do about it.

He woke sobbing and trembling all over. Why was he having such bad dreams? He knew the war was causing many people to have bad dreams, but his seemed to be more constant.

His family didn't seem to wake up soaked with sweat every night the way he was. He went to the kitchen and gulped down a glass of water. He drank a second glass just as fast. But with the third glass he walked to the sofa and, holding the glass with still trembling hands carefully lowered it to the coffee table. He sat down and rubbed the cool glass along his forehead, down his cheeks and down his neck. He took deep breaths and let them out slowly. Counting to three each time he released the breath.

After what seemed like an hour, his heart was down to an easy rhythm and he'd stopped shaking. He sipped the water and leaned his head against the back of the sofa. Maybe all he needed was more exercise. He opened the balcony door and stepped out into the cool desert air. Over the smell of fried garlic from a nearby restaurant and gas fumes, he thought he caught of whiff of sea air.

Like his mother, Jonathon loved the ocean. He understood her thirst for long distance swimming. It was her solace for everyday troubles.

It may upset lifeguards at the beach, but Jonathon could feel Mom's joy as she swam away from the crowds. And he wished he could swim all the way across the Pacific to where ever his father was right now. Even if Dad were in the midst a raging gun battle against the enemy, at least he was doing something. But Jonathon couldn't get rid of the feeling that his dad was close by.

Jonathon sat out on the balcony, soothed by water whispering against the concrete sides of the pool. The smell of the chlorine was pungent, but somehow comforting.

Suddenly, Jonathon was overwhelmed with sleepiness. Maybe this time he could sleep without bad dreams. He walked back into the living room and stretched on the sofa. No sense in waking his brothers.

He finally found a comfortable position with his head and torso on the seat and his legs raised up over the back of the sofa. He might regret the position in the morning, but right now it felt great.

He fell asleep and not a dream, not even an image entered his slumber. Three hours later, he was awakened by the sound of someone moving around in the kitchen. He heard water running and filling up what was probably the coffee pot. Then he heard the gas stove click on and the ping of metal against metal as someone scooped coffee from the can into the strainer for the grounds.

He heard Richard's tenor voice hum a tune, "Happy Days Are Here Again." Wishful thinking on his brother's part.

Jonathon slid his legs down to the floor and pushed against the sofa cushions to stand up. His back creaked but when he was fully upright, he felt good. No cricks at all in his back. Maybe he'd sleep like that more often.

He walked into the kitchen and nodded at his brother, who was leaning against the kitchen counter sipping his coffee. "You off to work soon? Jonathon asked.

Richard nodded. "Yeah they have great doughnuts in the breakroom."

"I know you think I'm being silly about the baseball card, but..."

Richard interrupted him with a shake of his head. "Actually, I don't think you're being silly. And I will ask." He put his cup in the sink and ran some water in it, so the coffee dregs wouldn't stain it. On his way out of the room, he squeezed his brother's arm. "We'll get through this."

"I hope so," said Jonathon. Richard was shutting the front door as Jonathon opened the bathroom door. He wondered what time it was. It seemed early still.

Done with the bathroom, he headed down the hall to his bedroom. But the creak of a door opening caught his attention. He turned back toward the living room, expecting to see Richard coming back in.

He opened his mouth to ask if Richard had forgotten something, but shut it immediately when he realized the person coming in was much shorter. Short enough to be a midget. "Mr. Jungen? What are you doing here?" shouted Jonathon.

Chapter 28

MR. JUNGEN PUT HIS finger to his lips. "Shhh! he whispered. "Don't wake up your family." He beckoned for Jonathon to come with him as he headed for the sofa.

Mouth open and breath coming hard, Jonathon followed. But he didn't sit next to the man. He stood towering over him, glowering down at the midget. "Explain yourself now, or I will wake everybody in this building up."

"Calm down, Jonathon. Calm down."

Jonathon shook his head and crossed his arms over this chest. "No, I won't calm down. Explain yourself."

"Come sit beside me and I'll tell you."

Jonathon looked at his watch. "You've got 5 seconds to start explaining."

The man looked at him with sad eyes. "This would be…"

"Five!"

"Okay, okay." Mr. Jungen sighed. "Herr Hitler really came to everyone's attention in 1933, but he'd been wiggling his way into a dominant position earlier than that. And some of us took notice."

"What's that got to do with what's going on here with my family?"

"I'll get to that, but I have to set the stage." Mr. Jungen patted the seat next to him again. "Please Jonathon, I'm getting a crick in my neck looking up at you."

Jonathon sat in the overstuffed chair opposite the sofa. But he sat on the very edge, his legs tensed to push him upright if need be.

Mr. Jungen sat back half way. "What I told you earlier about being sent to this country at an early age is true. Well, partly true. We were sent here as young teens to learn to speak English fluently with an American accent."

"Wait a minute! Didn't you tell us that Dr. Ringwaldt got his PhD from Leipzig? Did he go back to Germany?"

The little guy nodded. "Yes, he did go back for college, and really did want to study earthquakes here. So it was plausible for him to come back in his twenties."

Jonathon nodded. "Okay, but what does that have to do with us?"

"Originally we were being trained to spy on Americans who might want to overthrow the Weimar Republic. Germany wasn't really trustful of the U.S. after losing the first world war."

"I'm waiting," said Jonathon.

"Long story short, then. When some of our leaders realized Hitler was destined to rule, they decided we would be more useful spying on Hitler enthusiasts. So, we began to look for those people. Not just Americans, but fellow transplanted Germans. Or first and second generation German-Americans. We were spread out across the countries and hired into many industries." He puffed out his chest and grinned. "I really am a Fuller Brush Man and proud of it."

Jonathon relaxed his legs at bit. "Go on. What were you supposed to do if you found Nazi sympathizers?"

"Report them to our handlers."

"How did you do that?"

Mr. Jungen nodded. "That's the hard part, but we have developed ways." He smiled. "Including members in your secret intelligence organization. You know? The service your dad and now your brother work for."

"No, Dad's a Marine," Jonathon said shaking his head. *Or is he?*

"I'm sorry. I just assumed you knew who employed them."

"Get on with your story. I'm not going to let you distract me this time."

Mr. Jungen nodded. "Recently, we'd discovered that two or three of our little group had been compromised and were now secretly working for the Third Reich. Revealing what the rest of us had learned." He ran his hand across his face. "That's why Bruno and your other neighbor, G, were murdered."

Jonathon stared at the little man. "You mean they were working for the Nazis'?

"No! Absolutely not!" cried Mr. Jungen. "The Nazis killed them and tried to find the information they were gathering." He shook his head. "We don't think Nazis found the information, but we can't be sure." He held his hands out, palms up. "The problem is, we don't know what the information was or where they hid it."

"Is that why you've been sneaking into our house and keeping watch on us?"

"Yes and no."

"Explain," growled Jonathon. "I'm tired of your secrecy. You owe us answers."

But before Mr. Jungen could answer Mom appeared. She was standing by the dining table holding a rolling pin up in the air like a cudgel. "Yes indeed, Mr. Jungen. I would like to hear your answer as well. I assume you snuck by my son to get in. But you will tell us what you're up to right now."

He nodded and placed his hands on his knees. "Please be seated, Mrs. Thomas. I was just about to tell Jonathon I snuck into your house the other day to see if I could find anything in your den or Jonathon's room that Bruno might have given him."

"Why would you think Dr. Ringwaldt gave me anything?"

"Because he was quite fond of you. He imagined if he'd had any children, his son would be like you. And you shared his love for the game of baseball. It was his favorite sport, even more than soccer."

"What would he have given me?" asked Jonathon, keeping his face muscles as still as he could in the hopes Mr. Jungen wouldn't figure out about the Babe Ruth card.

"That's the problem." Mr. Jungen shrugged. "I have no idea."

"Well, why did you abduct me yesterday?"

"I wasn't abducting you. I was going to drop you off here."

"Oh yeah, that's why you had Mr. Gorilla push me into the car."

"Yes. In part because I didn't think you'd come willingly."

"That's exactly right. Don't know why I should trust you."

The small man nodded. "I can understand that. But the other reason was we wanted it to look like we were kidnapping you was to throw off the two men who were tailing you on foot."

"Somebody was tailing me?"

Mr. Jungen nodded.

"Not possible. I was super careful."

"As much as you could be. But you're not trained to avoid being seen."

"And you're hard to miss, Jonathon," said Mom.

"And you weren't expecting to be followed."

"Okay, I get it." Jonathon's shoulder's slumped. "But I still don't understand why Dr. Ringwaldt was stabbed. Or what Mr. Schmidt was doing in our house."

"We don't know yet, but I think Bruno was killed because he wouldn't reveal where he'd hidden the information."

"Okay. So, it was just coincidence that Richard and I found him?"

"Yah, probably." The midget nodded.

"But, what about Mr. Schmidt? What was he doing in our house? And why was he murdered?"

"We don't know for certain, but we think he was looking for Bruno's information and he was followed by someone who wanted what he'd found."

"He found something in our house? What?"

"That I don't know. It's why I came to see you."

"I don't know anything!" Jonathon slapped the side of his chair. "I'm just a high school student. What could I possibly know?"

"You probably don't even realize you know something. Did Bruno ever give you something? Anything?"

"Like what?"

"I don't know. A special post card he'd gotten on a trip?"

Jonathon wondered if he should tell Mr. Jungen about the Babe Ruth card, but he still didn't trust the man.

"No. No post cards. Nothing I can remember having any messages."

"I need to get going," said Mr. Jungen, standing up. "If you remember anything, please call your police contact."

"Why them? Why not the secrets people?"

"Because we think that's where the leak is."

The man moved toward the front door, but Jonathon walked right beside him. Just to make sure he went out the door and not toward the bedrooms.

When Mr. Jungen was fully out of the apartment and the front door was shut behind him, Jonathon locked it and fastened the security chain. He stood in front of it, sure they hadn't seen the last of the small man.

"That man gives me the creeps," he said, turning to look at his mother.

She nodded. "Is that why you didn't…"

Jonathon put his finger to his lips. "Let's wait a while before we say anything. And then we're only going to discuss casual stuff," he whispered.

Chapter 29

M OM TURNED TOWARD THE kitchen. "I'm going to make some coffee. Would you like some?"

Jonathon nodded. "That would be nice. Shall I make breakfast?"

"I'm not really hungry yet, thank you dear." She dumped the old coffee grounds out and rinsed the pot. While she finished making the coffee, she said, "I'm just going to brush my teeth and wash my face. Then I'm going to drink my coffee and see what I can plan for us to do today."

Jonathon nodded and pulled a piece of paper out of his notebook. 'I'm going to see if Mr. Jungen left anything behind in the living room. I don't want him to have any excuse to come back.' he wrote.

Mom wrote back, 'good idea'. She turned and went into the bathroom.

Jonathon went to his bedroom to pick up his Calculus book. He might as well study that too. Get ahead of his class as best he could.

Christopher was just sitting up in his bed and stretching his arms above his head. "I thought I heard voices a little earlier. Was someone visiting?"

"You probably heard me talking with Mom."

Christopher shook his head. "No, sounded like a man's voice."

"I was talking with Richard before he left for work. Maybe that's what you heard."

Christopher narrowed his eyes and furrowed his brow. "Maybe."

But he didn't look convinced.

"I think Mom will let me go for a swim today. You got time after your studies to go with me?"

"Sure."

"Maybe we can talk Mom into coming and play four-person water polo, or something. I'm sure our mermaid sister will want to play."

Christopher rumbled a laugh and grabbed his clothes. "Sounds like fun."

After his brother left the room, Jonathon pulled out another sheaf of paper and drew a line down the middle. "What I Know" was the heading for the left column. "Questions to be answers," was the heading for the right-hand column.

He stared at the left-hand column, pencil poised to write down what he knew. But what did he know? Anything? Yes. "Somebody is out to get us."

In the question column he wrote, "Who?"

Back to the *I know* column he wrote, "Mr. Jungen tried to kidnap me."

"But did he really? Or was he trying to save me?" went in the *Questions* column.

"Dad's in the Marines."

"Or is he in this secret organization?"

Back and forth he went and when his hand started to cramp, he looked down and recognized that to every single thing he had in the *I know* column, he had a least three questions in the negative column.

How was he ever going to solve the problem and get them back home? Especially stuck in here?

But he knew he'd not be able to sneak out again. Everybody would be watching out for him to do just that.

He wondered if he could find a way to ask Richard questions without his brother figuring out what was happening.

Probably not. But still it was worth a try. He stuck the paper back in the notebook. He put it in the middle so nobody would find it. But how would he be able to find it easily?

Dogearing would give away its position to anybody looking. He tried putting it in opposite of the other pages, so the back of it faced the front.

That was too obvious.

Maybe he could make a little mark on the rings that held the paper in. But with what?

Ah, his ink pen. He pulled the cap off that and put a dot of ink on the side of the center ring.

He smiled. Handy to be messy. Nobody would think twice if spotting it at all.

He was about to open his history book when his stomach growled. He looked at his watch and realized it was already ten o'clock. He hadn't had anything to eat.

When he opened the door into the hallway, he smelled the aroma of bacon and toast. He wondered if there was any left.

Sure enough, when he looked into the kitchen there was bacon in the frying pan and toast with jam waiting for him on the counter. The only good thing about being in this apartment was they seemed to have a never-ending supply of hard-to-find items.

Jonathon was surprised Mom didn't tell whoever brought the food to take it back and feed it to the soldiers in the hospitals. Maybe she didn't know whom to tell.

Of course, they'd only been there just over a day. Maybe they were about out of the good stuff. It would probably be back to oatmeal tomorrow.

He poured himself a cup of coffee and some orange juice. Of course, it wasn't fresh from their trees, but then it was the wrong time of year for that. Still, this made-from-frozen-concentrate juice was pretty good and it was nice to have orange juice all year long. Jonathon wondered what other things would come frozen in the future.

If there was a future. What if the Allied Forces didn't prevail? Would the West Coast become part of Japan? He'd eaten Japanese food before and it was okay, but he wasn't sure what they ate for breakfast. Miso soup didn't really strike his fancy and he figured they didn't eat fried eggs.

He took his coffee and juice out to the dining table and looked around to see where the rest of his family had gotten to. They weren't in the living room or out on the balcony and he felt his heart rate revving up. The bathroom? No, that door was open when he went by.

Maybe down by the pool. He rushed out to the balcony railing and looked over. Nobody there.

Were they in Mom's room? No!

The silence in the apartment was deafening. He looked for signs of a struggle, but Mom and Mary Anne's beds were neatly made and their toiletries were lined up in prefect order on the top of the dresser.

In his bedroom, there was order, well as much as guys could manage. Probably better than other males, since their military dad had drilled into their heads barracks neatness. They automatically made their beds with square corners and spreads so tight you could bounce a quarter off them. Of course, his and Christopher's homework papers were spread out over the surface.

Out of habit, Jonathon gathered up his papers, stacked them in a neat pile and laid them on a corner of the dresser. All the while, he was listening for sounds of his family.

Something was wrong. Why was the place so quiet? Almost as if no-one else lived there. That wasn't true. After all, somebody had made the coffee and toast and orange juice.

Jonathon's pulse throbbed in his temple and an ache in his neck was creeping upward toward his head. The start of a tension headache. Was he actually having another nightmare? Was he going to feel the apartment building shake? Somehow, this didn't feel like a dream.

He sat on the edge of his bed, closed his eyes and sucked in a deep breath. He held it as long as he could and slowly shushed it out his parted lips. He did that three more times and felt the ache in his head subside.

He shook out the tension in his arms and legs and twisted his neck from side to side. Feeling better, he rose from the bed and went back into the living room. Maybe Mom had left him a note.

Where would she leave it? Probably on the dining room table.

But he didn't see it on the top.

Maybe it fell into one of the chairs? No.

On the floor? No.

And there was no note anywhere in that area.

He moved over toward the sofa, but there was no note there. Either on the sofa, or in between the cushions or behind it.

He searched all around the coffee table and all around the overstuffed chair. No note.

He searched along the bookshelves and by the radio. No luck.

He sat down on the floor to get a different perspective on the room and to slow his heart down again.

Surely, he was just overlooking a clue.

He spread himself out flat on his front, nose just inches off the floor. It might have floated off a table and fallen under something. Inch by inch he scanned the room, forcing himself to take his time.

Nothing showed up other than dust bunnies the cleaning service had missed and stains on the carpet that nobody had noticed or done anything about.

Then he caught sight of something beige peeking out from under the sofa. He'd missed it before, because it wouldn't have been visible under the upholstery skirt covering the legs.

Keeping flat on his stomach, he squirmed his way over, figuring he'd lose sight of it from an upright position. He inched it out until he felt resistance and reached his hand further under the sofa to see if he could feel where the paper was caught.

Part of it had slipped under the leg and was stuck. He gently wiggled it back and forth, pulling it from under the leg. After what seemed like an hour later, he worked the page loose.

He sat up and spread his legs out in front of him. It was a note from someone.

But no-one he knew.

Chapter 30

MAYBE IT WAS LEFT over from the last tenant. He was about to crumble it up to throw away, but one last look made him drop the paper.

It had his name on it! At the top, printed in all caps, it said: Important!

Definitely not from Mom or the twins or Richard.

Wait a minute. The handwriting does look a bit familiar. Almost like how he remembered his dad's handwriting.

Why would Dad be writing him a letter and delivering like this?

And who delivered it?

Not Dad. Couldn't be, right?

Maybe that's what Mr. Jungen was doing here earlier.

But why didn't he just say so? Why be so secretive?

He was just about to read the thing when he heard the key scrape in the lock. He jumped up, whipped around behind the sofa and peered out from around the edge.

It was probably just his family coming back from where ever they'd gone. Without him, he grumped to himself.

But what if it wasn't they? What would he do then?

He looked around for something he could throw.

Nothing. He wasn't close enough to the bookshelves to grab a book.

The only thing to do would be to launch himself at an intruder, fists ready to punch him in the eye, and head ready to butt him in the gut.

He tensed himself for the launch and quivered in anticipation.

But then he heard Mary Anne giggle at something Christopher was saying and Jonathon's muscles relaxed into what felt like a puddle of melting butter.

He pulled himself around the sofa's side and up onto one of the cushions. He leaned back, crossed his legs and spread his arms along the top. Relaxed he did not feel, but he was darned if he was going to let his family know they'd scared him.

Probably Mom just trying to let him know how she'd felt yesterday.

When she appeared through the just opened doorway, Jonathon smiled and asked, "Where've you been?"

Mom's eyes widened. "Oh Honey! Didn't you get my note?"

Mary Anne smirked. "I threw the note away. Figured it would do him good to worry about us for a change."

"That was an awful thing to do, Mary Anne." Mom scowled. "We were down in the laundry room."

Jonathon waved the paper he'd found. "Well, I'm glad you're back safe and sound. Look what was under the sofa."

"What?" They all asked at once.

He stood up and handed the page to Mom. "Doesn't that look like Dad's handwriting?"

Mom grabbed the paper as Christopher and Mary Anne crowded around her. "Yes, it does!" She looked up at Jonathon. "Where did you find this?"

"I was looking for a note from you and when I got on the floor to look, I saw this." He took the note back from his mother and laid it on the dining room table. "I haven't read it yet, but it is addressed to me." He pointed at the heading. And then he saw, *Jonathon's eyes only.*

He snatched it up and held it to his chest.

"What'd you do that for," asked Christopher.

"Put it back down, so we all can read it," ordered Mom.

"It says for my eyes only. I'll read and let you know what it says." He shook his head and stepped back as Mom reached for the paper. "That is if I'm allowed to."

Mom scowled, but Jonathon just shrugged and headed to his bedroom.

Jonathon, read the first line, *Yes, this is from me. Your dad. I am back in the States, but I can't be at home. It would put you all in harm's way.* Jonathon continued to read as his father told him that Mr. Jungen and Dr. Ringwaldt's group had indeed discovered a plot to overthrow the government and divide the country in half. They had pinpointed who the culprits were and had let some members of the secret service know. That's why Dad was back home.

According to Dad, Dr. Ringwaldt discovered that there was a spy embedded in the local branch of the agency and was in the process of trying to figure out who that was when he was murdered. *Guess, in a way, he had found out, huh Dad?* Jonathon thought.

But Jonathon still had his doubts the note really was from his dad. How did it get into the apartment? At least one member in the family had been there the whole time.

And why had he written this note to Jonathon? What could he do about what Dad had written? He was stuck in this apartment.

Why couldn't he tell his family? As far as he could tell there was nothing in the note that would endanger them anymore. And Dad hadn't specifically ordered him not to tell everybody else.

Plus, what if whoever wrote this note wanted to Jonathon to leave the building by himself to be kidnapped again.

He looked at his watch, realizing he was hungry. It was already noon. The bacon and toast hadn't lasted long for his metabolism.

This time, when he came out of his room, Mom was in the kitchen and the twins were studying at the dining table.

He stopped in the kitchen doorway, handed his mother the note. "I guess this is from Dad, but I don't know why he'd want for only me to read it."

She nodded and took the piece of paper. "It does look like his writing."

"But how did it get in our apartment?" Jonathon asked.

"Where did you say you found it?"

"Under the sofa."

"Wonder how it got there?"

Jonathon shook his head. "I don't know. I figured whoever left it, dropped it and then forgot about it."

Mom raised her left eyebrow and cocked her head to the side. Something she did when things didn't make sense to her.

"But who? And why?"

Jonathon shrugged. "Beats me." He stepped around his mother and opened the refrigerator. "When can we get one of these for our house? That icebox is so messy," he asked.

Mom smiled. "Soon, I hope. I'm saving up money as best I can to afford one."

"Great. May I make a sandwich? I haven't had much to eat today. I'll be happy to make sandwiches for everybody, if you'd like."

"Don't you have school work to do?" asked Mom. "You do that. I'm already making sandwiches." She pointed to the mayonnaise, lettuce and tomatoes she had set on the counter.

Jonathon decided he was most ready to study history. At the moment his class was in the midst of studying what caused the Civil War. He'd been taught that slavery was the main reason. And he agreed that enslaving another human being was wrong, but there had been slavery going on forever. All you had to do was read the Bible to see instances of one group of people enslaving another group.

Wasn't that one of the things that Hitler was doing with the Jews? How about the peoples of the countries the Romans conquered? Weren't some of them forced into slavery? Why?

And why were peoples like the Negroes and Indians more often forced into slavery than white people? Because of their skin color?

Jonathon shook his head and ran his hand over his hair. What was he supposed to do about it? He was still considered a kid. It wasn't his place to change the world.

He read two chapters in his history book. The first telling of President Lincoln's decision to wage war.

The second chapter dealt with some of the early battles. Jonathon remembered visiting relatives in Gettysburg, Pennsylvania, when he was about nine or ten. He tried to imagine how many men and boys lost their lives that day. That was toward the end of the war. How many small battles were there leading up to that day? And how many battles were now being fought all over Europe and the Pacific Islands killing more men and boys.

Plus, what about all the people who just happened to live in the contested areas? How many of them were trying to survive with no interest or say in what the warriors wanted or were doing?

He read the questions over at the back of each chapter and then answered them. But some of the questions troubled him and what he thought the correct answers were didn't make sense.

Yes, what Hitler, Mussolini, and Hirohito were doing was wrong. But what about the Allied Forces? Did they have anything to do with starting this war? Could they have behaved differently and prevented this war?

Jonathon sighed and closed his book. He needed to get some exercise. After all, they did have gym class every day at school. As he left his bedroom, he heard his mother announce that lunch was ready and tell Mary Anne to set the table.

"Why do I always have to do that?"

Christopher and Jonathon smiled at each other declaring, "Because you're the girl. That's a girl's job!"

"Not fair." Mary Anne, stuck out her lower lip, gathered up the school work and stumped into the kitchen.

Mom came out of the kitchen, put her hands on her hips and cocked her head. "You know what? Mary Anne's right."

She looked at Christopher. "You get the placemats and napkins.

"Jonathon, get the silverware.

"And, Mary Anne, you bring out the glasses and pitcher of water."

Jonathon scowled at his sister. "Trouble maker."

Mary Anne grinned. "Yup."

After they'd eaten their sandwich and cookies, Mom asked, "Who's up for a water polo match?"

"I am," said Jonathon.

"Anything to get out of this apartment," said Christopher.

"Dibs for Mom as my partner," shouted Mary Anne.

Jonathon stacked up the plates and silverware, while Christopher took the glasses into the kitchen.

"Leave the dishes there, boys. We'll do them after the game."

Chapter 31

JONATHON AND CHRISTOPHER RUSHED to their room and changed into their swimsuits. Jonathon was the first one to the front door. "Hurry up everybody. I can't wait to get out of this apartment."

Mary Anne came out next, carry a small ball and her snorkel. *She always takes it with her when she's going to be in the water,* Jonathon thought.

"Do you still use your snorkel when you take a bath?"

Mary Anne grinned. "Sometimes."

"Why?"

"Practice makes perfect."

When Mom and Christopher joined them, Jonathon jerked opened the front door and raced down the hall yelling, "Last into the pool is a rotten egg!"

"Slow down, son," called his mother. "We'll all go down together."

When they were in the pool warming up for the game, Mom pulled Jonathon aside. "I've been thinking about that letter you found today." She frowned. "I know you want to go see if that really was from your dad. And I'd liked to know if he really is in the U.S."

Jonathon's eyes lit up. Was Mom going to let him leave this building?

But Mom seemed to know what he was thinking. She rested her hand on his shoulder. "But that doesn't mean I want you to go off halfcocked and sneak around town."

Jonathon's shoulders slumped.

Mom smiled at him. "Let's discuss this with Richard when he gets home from work. See if we can come up with a solution and a way for you to investigate without being caught."

Christopher called to them from the other end of the pool. "Hey! Are we going to play or not?"

Mary Anne threw the ball at them.

For half an hour, the family tossed the ball around trying to get it across each other's goal line. Just as Mary Anne was about to throw the ball over her brothers' goal line, a heavy-set woman with dyed-blonde hair, a tight bathing suit, and high-heeled mules came prancing toward them.

"Yoo hoo," she yelled, pointing her finger at Mom. "This is a private pool for residents and this is my time to sun myself. You must stop this raucous behavior immediately and get out of the pool."

Mom signaled for Jonathon and the twins to move to the side of the pool. "I'm sorry, ma'am. I didn't see any sign reserving the pool for your private use. Please forgive us. My children were just taking a break from doing school work."

She put her foot on the pool ladder as if about to exit the pool. "If you show me where the sign indicating when people can reserve private pool time is, I'll be happy to sign up for a time and leave now."

Christopher nodded and headed for the ladder on the opposite of the pool. "We certainly wouldn't want to intrude on someone's private time."

The woman's bluster was fading out. "Well, it's not official that I have reserved this time, I just come around this time every day." She moved over to one of the lounge chairs and spread out her towel. "Carry on and I'll just sun myself here."

Jonathon gathered up the ball and hopped out of the pool. "That's alright, my sister and Mom were winning anyway."

The family gathered up their towels, slipped on their sandals, and headed toward the building's entrance.

Mary Anne and Christopher checked to see the woman was not watching and then, holding their pinkies in the air, sashayed into the building.

A loud "Hmmph" came from behind them.

"Guess she was watching," said Jonathon. He opened the door into the building, but stopped and held his hand up for his family to wait behind him.

"Go on in," urged Mom.

But Jonathon shook his head and put a finger to his lips. He pointed down the hall and then turned his thumb toward the hallway branching off to the right. He tapped his ear and tilted his head slightly to the right. Then he made a walking motion with his middle two fingers on his right hand.

He put his hand up toward his family to make them stand still. Then inched his way down toward the second hallway, with his back to the wall. He stopped at the intersection, listened for a minute or two and then ducked his head around the corner. Nobody there and no apartment doors open at all.

He stepped into the middle of the hall and turned toward his family. Just as he opened his mouth to give the all clear, his mother shouted "Watch out! There's someone behind you.!"

But that was all the warning he got before whoever was behind him clamped a meaty hand over his mouth and put a knee into the back of Jonathon's knee. Before he had a chance to react, the person conked him on the head and Jonathon crumpled to the floor.

He woke up trussed to his bed with his heels and his hands inches apart behind his back. His head screamed in pain and he could hardly open his eyes.

Christopher was tied to his own bed, his eyes wide with fright. Mom and Mary Anne were lying on Richard's bed also tied up.

A man, at least three inches taller than Jonathon and a good forty pounds heavier was sitting in front of the door, tilting the chair back toward the wall.

Jonathon wondered how long it would be before the chair legs crumbled under the man's weight. He opened his mouth to speak, but the man's scowl and low growl made him change his mind.

Mom and Mary Anne were lying back to back with their hands touching. Maybe they could loosen their bindings, but then what could they do? There was no way they could overpower the behemoth guarding the door. Wasn't that the same gorilla who was with Mr. Jungen yesterday?

How could Jonathon get them out of this predicament? And how could he warn Richard that he was walking into a trap.

He raised his head up and said, "Excuse me, sir?"

The giant snarled. "Do not speak," said the man with a thick accent. Sounded like the accent used by people in movies who were speaking English as if they were from Germany.

"Yes, but I have to use the toilet."

"Wait!"

"What if I can't hold it any longer?"

"Pee in your pants," said the man with a sneer.

Mom piped up then. "That's cruel. And I'm pretty sure against the Geneva Convention rules."

"I don't care."

"You'll have the rest of us as hostages, what makes you think my brother would leave us in trouble?" asked Christopher.

Someone knocked on the door just then and Mr. Humongous rocked his chair back to all four legs. He stood up, faced the door and bellowed, "Who is it?"

"Helmut," came the tenor voice of the midget. "Who'd you think it was? And where are the Thomases?"

"In here." The big man opened the door a crack. "I am guarding them in here."

Mr. Jungen's mouth fell open as he entered the room. "What do you mean by tying them up like this?" He rushed over to Jonathon's mom and sister and began to untie them.

"You told me to guard them," said the giant.

"For heaven's sake, Johann. Guard them, yes. Not make them prisoners." Mr. Jungen shook his head as he helped Mom sit up.

He pointed at Jonathon and Christopher. "Untie those boys right now. I'm so sorry, Mrs. Thomas. What that man does well is be big and strong."

"Thinking is not his long suit, I gather," said Mom rubbing her wrists and leaning forward to stretch her back.

After they were all comfortably seated in the living room and everyone had a beverage, Jonathon asked. "What's going on that we need more protection?"

"And why you?" asked Mom.

As Mr. Jungen opened his mouth to answer, there was a bump outside the front door. He put his forefinger to his lips and motioned for the family to hide behind the sofa.

But before they could move, the key scraped in the door and it creak open. Johann held his gun in front of him, ready to pull the trigger and Mr. Jungen stood in front of Mom, as if to guard her.

Whoever it was come very slowly, showing no sign of his body. The door was opened just enough for a foot sheathed in an ox-blood-colored penny loafer to appear. Then door stopped moving and Jonathon could hear muffled breathing.

Mr. Jungen counted to five and was just about to pounce forward, when the door swung fully open.

"Richard," cried Mom. "Why didn't you just come in? You scared us half to death."

"Sorry Mother," he said. "I wasn't sure Mr. Jungen had gotten our message. I didn't want to walk into a trap."

Chapter 32

"WHAT'S GOING ON?" ASKED Jonathon, as he stood up.

"Why are Mr. Jungen and the gorilla here?" asked Christopher.

"To protect you," said a man who had just come in behind Richard.

Mom's face flushed and her smile almost cut her face in half. "Paul! Is that really you?"

Jonathon and the twins weren't so sure. They were a year older than the last time they'd seen their dad. They didn't trust their memories. But when Mary Anne looked back and forth between Jonathon and the man, she squealed, "Daddy. It really is you!" She launched herself at him, forcing him to stagger backward before he could support her weight.

Dad looked over her head and smiled at Mom, his eyes lighting up with joy. "Hey, Blondie. I've missed you so much."

He set Mary Anne back onto her feet and reached Mom in one stride. He swept her up into his arms and spun her around. Then he bent her almost double as he kissed her solidly on the lips. When they came up for air, he spun them both around and sat on the sofa with Mom in his lap.

"Sit down, my family. And let me tell you a tale."

Mr. Jungen and Gustav started toward the door, but Dad said. "No, no, you two. You deserve to hear this, as well. Find a chair. Boys, why don't you and Mary Anne sit on the floor."

Richard scowled at being called a boy.

Jonathon could understand his brother's feelings. After all, he was probably working in the same outfit as Dad. But it was so good to be an almost complete family again, Jonathon figured Richard would let it slide.

Suddenly, Jonathon felt Caroline's absence. When would he see her again?

Dad's next comment brought Jonathon back to the present. "At the beginning of the year, just after we got into this war, I was doing some investigating in the Samoan islands. Checking how many Japanese sympathizers were there, I got hold of some information about a group of Nazi sympathizers there." Dad stopped to sip some water.

"How did Nazi's get to islands in the Pacific?" asked Christopher. "What do they have to do with German interests?"

"Hitler and Hirohito are working together, so maybe they were there to recruit support from other nations," said Jonathon.

"Good assumption," said Dad. "The problem is the Japs aren't very popular amongst the islanders. And not just the islanders. The Koreans hate the Japanese's guts."

"Why?" asked Mary Anne.

"Because the Japs are kidnapping their people and using them for slave labor," said Richard.

"What do we care?" asked Christopher. "They're all slanty-eyed idiots."

"Christopher Miner Thomas! How dare you lump people together like that!" Mom's eyes flashed like lightning.

"Well, that's what everybody says at school." Christopher slumped his shoulders and picked at his toenails.

"They all look the same, if you ask me," said Jonathon.

Mom sighed. "Well, we just need to pay closer attention to see the differences."

"Anyway," said Dad. "This cell of German spies is trying to disrupt the American Samoan government and put a Nazi sympathizer in charge."

"Wait a minute, these islands are ours?" asked Jonathon. "I didn't know we owned land in the Pacific Ocean."

"We don't actually own it, but it is under our protection," said Dad. "How about you let me finish my story without interruptions."

He waited until his family had settled down and continued. "I broke into one of the German's houses and searched for documents. That's when I found correspondence having to do with our neighbor, Bruno Ringwaldt."

Mom slid off Dad's lap and sat next to him on the sofa. She picked at the cuticles on her fingers and sighed.

Dad patted her hand and continued. "Fortunately, one of the young fellows with me was fluent in German and was able to translate on the spot. Unfortunately, that's what got him killed. This group has a faction here and they were discussing what to do about Bruno and Helmut and the others who are trying to keep the Nazis from taking over the U.S." He shook his head and looked sadly at Mr. Jungen.

"I know Bruno was a good friend of yours, Helmut, and I'm sorry for your loss." The midget nodded and blew into his handkerchief.

"Anyway, the OSS decided I should come home secretly and investigate who was operating in this country," he ran a hand over his close-cropped hair, the new GI look. "I can't tell you how hard it's been not to get in touch with you all."

"That would have been dangerous for us, wouldn't it?" Jonathon said.

Dad nodded. "It helped that Bruno and Helmut were in the neighborhood."

"That's why you saw my Studebaker in Bruno's driveway the other day. We were discussing how to keep you safe." Mr. Jungen said.

"But why did you break into our house and then run away?" asked Mom.

"I thought you'd be asleep and that I could find Jonathon's baseball card collection in the den."

"What's so important about my cards?"

"Bruno was making notes on some cards that he kept and he gave you the Babe Ruth one by mistake."

"Oh, that's one of my most favorite cards."

The midget smiled and nodded. "He knew that and didn't have the heart to ask for it back. We thought if I could just switch it for a different version of the same card, you'd never notice the difference."

"But I saw you take my whole collection the other day, Dad." Jonathon paused and looked at his father. "That was you at our house, right?"

Dad nodded. "That's why Gnter Schmidt was in the house when he was murdered. He agreed to find the card, but he must have been followed by the Nazis. They murdered him to take the card."

Jonathon raised his hand. "Dad…"

Dad held up his hand and shook his head at Jonathon. "No, son. He didn't have the cards on him when we found his body."

"So, who are these Krauts?" asked Christopher. When he saw Mr. Jungen and Mr. Muller shudder at the name, he looked surprised. "I'm sorry, is that not a nice word?"

"No, it is not." said Mr. Muller, "It was used by the Americans and the British as derogatory term during the first world war."

"Won't use it again," mumbled Christopher, hanging his head.

"Wait a minute," said Jonathon, "I remember Jennifer's neighbor making a snide comment about Dr. Ringwaldt last week when I was visiting her."

"What did he say?" asked Dad.

"Jennifer's dad invited Mr. Englemann to a party to show other friends that not all Germans were Nazis. He told him that Dr. Ringwaldt was coming. Mr. Englemann, actually spat on the sidewalk and said he wouldn't be seen in the same place as Dr. Ringwaldt."

"It may be something else all together but it's sure worth checking out." Dad smiled and patted Jonathon's shoulder. "Thanks, son."

"Let's take a break and let you all change out of your swim clothes." Dad looked at Mary Anne. "How about you gather up your clothes and change in the bathroom so I can spend some time alone with your mother."

"Is anybody getting hungry?" asked Jonathon. "How about I make grilled cheese sandwiches after I change?"

Christopher patted his stomach after he stood up. "I'll help."

Richard said, "Sounds good to me. I'd help but I've got to pack some clothes. I won't be around for a while."

"Where are you going?" asked Mary Anne, coming back into the room after getting her clothes.

Mr. Jungen and the gorilla stood up. "We're leaving," said Mr. Jungen. We'll have your dad brief us tomorrow."

"Are you sure?" asked Richard.

"You're welcome to stay," said Christopher as he walked back into the room.

The now-considered-to-be-friendly giant, smiled and said "*danke*. I think it is time for us to leave."

Dad came out of the bedroom and said. "No. Wait. Have something to eat and we'll all go together."

Chapter 33

"THAT'S NOT SAFE," SAID Mr. Jungen. "Four men leaving together would raise eyebrows."

Dad paused and nodded. "You're right. Let's eat something, then Helmut, you and I will leave" He pointed at Richard. "You and Johann will leave half an hour later. We'll meet at our usual rendezvous at dusk. Around 9 p.m."

Jonathon smiled as he remembered how late it was when it turned dark outside. The only good thing that came out of this war was "War Time."

"I'll give you guys the first grilled cheese sandwiches, so you'll be ready to go."

After the four men had eaten, Jonathon started on sandwiches for the rest of the family.

Christopher took over cooking duties when Dad beckoned for Richard and Jonathon to follow him into the boys' bedroom.

Dad shut the door and listened for anybody else's footsteps. When he was certain nobody else was listening, he said "I'm afraid to let those two out of our sight. "I don't want them to upset the apple cart and capture or kill Karl Englemann before we round up the whole spy ring.

He turned toward Jonathon. "Your mom's not happy about this, but I want you to go visit Jennifer tomorrow after school."

"What if she's not speaking to me? What do I do then?"

"Why wouldn't she speak to you?" asked Richard.

"I haven't talked with her since Sunday afternoon."

"Tell her Mary Anne came down with a bad infection in her lungs and the doctor thought it might contagious."

"But she's all better now?"

Dad nodded. "Or he ran a culture and determined it wasn't going to affect anybody else."

Jonathon hung his head. "She's probably not going to believe me, but I'll try."

Richard ruffled his brother's hair. "Sweet talker like you can make her believe you."

Jonathon grimaced. "Should I meet her at school or at her house?"

"Her house would be better, I think," said Dad. "But keep an eye out for Mr. Englemann."

"What am I supposed to ask her?"

Dad said, "I'm really concerned about what her neighbor, Karl Englemann, has been up to. Has she seen strange cars at his house? Has his son, um...Kurt? asked her about Bruno Ringwaldt? Things that seem out of the ordinary."

"What if she wants to know why I'm asking? What do I do then?"

"Be vague," said Richard, "but tell her you'd heard rumors about him."

Jonathon shrugged his shoulders. "I'll try."

Dad gave Jonathon a hug and Richard gently punched him on the arm.

After Dad hugged the rest of family, saying things like "Christopher give Mary Anne a break," and "Mary Anne listen to your mother," and "My darling blonde, I miss you so much," which made everybody else roll his eyes, he and Mr. Jungen slipped out the front door, after making sure the coast was clear.

Mom kept hugging Richard, then going off to clean something, and then coming back to hug him again. Finally, he said, "Okay, okay, Mom. I promise you I'm being extra careful.

He checked his watch again and smiled at Mr. Muller, "Our turn," He waved at Mom and the twins and winked at Jonathon. Then the two left just as quietly as Dad and Mr. Jungen had.

Jonathon wasn't sure the rest of the day would ever past. He worked on his chemistry assignment, but that didn't take long.

He worked on his Latin assignment, but was bored silly.

When Mom announce she was going to bed, she said "And I think the rest of you should go to bed as well."

"But I'm not tired yet," said Christopher.

"Neither am I," said Jonathon. "May we just play a game until we get sleepy?'

Mom smiled. "Just be quiet while you play."

"Yeah, don't wake me up," said Mary Anne, with a wink.

When the boys were alone, Christopher asked, "Are you going out tomorrow?"

Jonathon nodded.

"Can I go with you?"

Jonathon shook his head. "I think it's better if you stay here to guard Mom and Mary Anne."

Christopher dealt out cards for a game of 500 rummy and set down almost all his cards on his first turn. His smirk made Jonathon laugh. "Just you wait, brother mine. This game is not over yet." He put down the king and eight on Christopher's line of spades and the final four on Christopher' pile.

And then Christopher was up to three cards because he had to draw one and couldn't use any.

Soon, Christopher was up to six cards and Jonathon was down to two. The game went on until midnight, when Christopher, with a triumphant "Ha Ha!" slapped down his last three cards.

"Good game!" Jonathon added up the points left in his hand. "Add fifty more points to your total."

Christopher put down the scores while Jonathon gathered the cards and started to shuffle. "Do you want to play again, Christopher?"

"No, I'm beat."

"I'm still wide awake. I think I'll read for a while."

"You can read in our bedroom," said Christopher. "I'm used to sleeping with the light on."

"Thanks, I'll just stay out here. I'm feeling very jittery." After Christopher left, Jonathon poured a glass of water and set his notebook on the dining table. He wrote down a list of what he wanted to ask Jennifer about her neighbor. At least he started to write down a list, but images of being close to her kept interrupting his train of thought.

Would she smell as good as she used to? Would her hair glisten the way it did the last time he saw her? Jonathon smiled and shook his head. Of course she would. It'd only been a few days since he'd seen here. It just felt like years.

He shook his head to clear it. Then he wrote: 1. Has Mr. E been as friendly as he had been before the comment about Dr. Ringwaldt? 2. Had there been a funeral for Dr. Ringwaldt? 3. Had there been a write up in the paper?

Jonathon put his pencil down. When was the last time he'd seen the paper? Sunday morning, he guessed. And what day was it now?

He leaned back in his chair and tried to visualize the days. Sunday, they went to the beach and he met that girl; what was her name? Gloria. She was nice, but not as nice as Jennifer.

Let's see, he thought, when they'd gotten home that day, the police were already there. Jonathon sat upright in his chair. Wait a minute! How did the police know to come to his house? Had Dad been there?

Then Jonathon's mouth dropped open and he whispered, "Did Dad kill Mr. Schmidt?"

He shook his head and shuddered, "No. Not possible."

He still didn't understand how the man had gotten into the house. After the incident with Mr. Jungen, Mom and Mary Anne had gone around and locked all the windows. Plus, Jonathon and Christopher had gone around the outside of the house removing anything that could be climbed on from under the windows.

Did Dad give him a key to get in? To look for the baseball card? That could be, but why wouldn't Dad just go himself?

Jonathon was glad he hadn't, because if he had, Dad might be dead. Unless he was the murderer. *No, not possible.*

And wasn't Mr. Schmidt on our side? Wasn't he one of the good guys? Jonathon's head was throbbing. He couldn't even think straight, and he wasn't sure he could sleep.

He probably should try anyway. He looked at his watch. It was two a.m. and he had to get some sleep. He inched the bedroom door open, trying not to make a sound. Christopher was bunched up against the wall, his knees bent almost double. His breath puffed out in flutters. Most definitely asleep, thought Jonathon.

He slipped off his trousers and shirt and folded them over his shoes which he'd place by his bed. Then he eased his body in between the sheets and lay on his back staring up at the ceiling.

He was looking forward to seeing Jennifer and fell asleep dreaming of her violet eyes. In what seemed like a minute, he was jolted wide awake. He had his nightmare again, but this time he watched as Jennifer was swallowed up in the one of the chasms and then the rift had closed over her.

He glanced at his watch and realized it was already five a.m. But the image of the dream wouldn't leave his head. Was his brain telling him he was putting Jennifer in harm's way? Should he not go see her? Could he keep her safe?

A glance at his brother confirmed that Christopher was still sound asleep. How could he sleep that well at such a scary time?

Jonathon got up and pulled back a corner of the blackout curtain hiding their window. It was still dark outside, but golden rays from the sun were peering over the horizon. He slipped out of the bedroom, clothes and shoes in his arms. He decided to work some more on his list of questions. Somehow, he seemed to feel he could ask Jennifer the questions and not get her too curious about what he was trying to learn. No sense in getting her in trouble. After all, she was friends with Mr. Englemann's son, Kurt.

Chapter 34

JONATHON AND KURT WERE in the same English and gym classes, but they didn't have much in common. Kurt stayed around with other boys who spoke German. Of course, he was born in Germany so he probably missed being there. Still, Jonathon thought Kurt would be better off if he only, or at least mostly, spoke English. To fit in better.

Jennifer thought Kurt was nice and wanted to make him feel at home. She also was friends with Japanese children, and was very upset when they were sent off to internment camps. She didn't think it was fair that the Japanese living in the States should be lumped in with the people who started the war. She said most of her friends didn't even speak Japanese.

Jonathon agreed with what she said, though Kurt seemed different. Almost as if he didn't want to fit in.

But after the dream he'd just had, he didn't want to think about bad things. He just wanted school time to be over so he could see Jennifer. He missed her so much. He wondered how his parents dealt with not seeing each other. They always seemed so connected.

Jonathon moved into the kitchen to make a pot of coffee and maybe toast a piece of bread. He scraped the bottom of the coffee can to get enough grounds for a pot. It was mostly the chicory that had settled at the bottom of the can. Not his favorite flavor, but these days it was as close as it came to real coffee. There weren't enough slices of bread for everyone to have a piece, so Jonathon boiled water for oatmeal, again not a favorite of his but better than nothing and his stomach was growling.

By the time he'd finished his breakfast, Mom had come into the kitchen. She stroked his brow and asked, "Did you get any sleep at all, darling?"

He nodded. "Some. But I had that dream again."

"The one with the earthquakes?"

"Yep. This time Jennifer was swallowed up."

"Oh Jonathon. That must have been so scary."

He shrugged his shoulder and shuddered. "Yep. Am I doing the right thing, Mom?"

His mother looked at him with great sadness in her eyes. "I wish I could say yes for certain, but I can't."

"What do I do?"

"Do you trust that what your father asked of you is important?"

"Yes...yes, I do."

"Do you think Jennifer would want to help?"

"I guess so, but she doesn't like to think anybody is capable of evil. She probably won't believe me."

"She does understand that Hitler and Emperor Hirohito are bad men?" Mom nodded at her own question, "I'm sure she does. She's very bright and reads the newspapers."

"You're right about her being smart. She's even smarter than me."

"Jonathon, smarter than 'I' not smarter than 'me'."

"Sorry, wasn't thinking."

Mom hugged Jonathon and pulled his upper body down to her level to kiss his forehead. She opened the cabinets to look for breakfast food. "I sure hope they bring us our ration coupons today. We're almost out of food."

"I could buy food on the way home from Jennifer's. Then it would be like I was just doing regular errands."

"Excellent idea, honey, if we get the coupons. We can't buy anything without the coupons."

"Lots of people buy stuff on the black market. Maybe I could go there."

"Absolutely not. The black market is illegal and hurts the war effort. Would you rather eat fancy food or win this war?"

"Sorry, I wasn't thinking."

"Maybe you could swing by our house, since you'll be out, and pick up the mail."

"Um, okay, but wouldn't that alert people to the fact that we're still around?"

"Hmm, I don't know the answer to that."

"Well, let me know before I leave."

Jonathon pulled out his history book and read the next chapter on reconstruction after the Civil War. Carpetbaggers seemed only interested in bettering themselves and not helping people in the South at all.

If the Allied Forces lost the current war against Germany and Japan, would similar types come and make things even worse for the losing side? If Jonathon's side won, would they do the same to the losers? Was that just the way of war?

Jonathon hoped not. He hoped the winners would try to make life better for everybody. Probably just pie in the sky, he thought. As far as he could tell very few wars had really good outcomes for everybody.

And why couldn't the bad guys see how wrong they were? How did they get people to support them? Even the people who had moved to a different country for a better life? How come they supported the country they'd left?

People like Karl Englemann, why did they seem to take the Nazi's side? Why not just go back to Germany if they thought that side was in the right? He rubbed the top of his head again. He just wanted life to go back to normal, where people seemed to be happy and got along.

He smiled at Mary Anne as she sat down to eat her oatmeal. She looked as if she could have slept longer. "You feeling okay, Mary Anne? Did you not sleep well?"

She shook her head. "This waiting around in hiding is getting me down. I beginning to understand why you snuck out the other day."

Jonathon patted her hand. "Maybe this'll all be over soon and we can get back to normal."

"Whatever normal is. I don't think we'll be back to normal until this war is over and only if we win." She shook her head. "I can't imagine living under Nazi or Japanese rule."

Christopher came in with his oatmeal and said, "That wouldn't be the end. The Kra...oops Germans, and the Japs would start fighting each other and using us as their fighters until one of them took over the whole world."

"I'm glad you remembered Mr. Muller's reaction to your using Kraut," Mom said.

Christopher smiled. "Actually, the giant isn't a bad guy once you get to know him."

"What with him and the midget, Mr. Jungen, I wonder if we've joined the circus," muttered Jonathon.

"Yeah," said Mary Anne, "is that all they can recruit? Misfits?"

"They both strike me as good-hearted men, despite their sizes. After all, Mr. Muller's only three inches taller than Jonathon."

"But three times bigger than I across the chest. The man is huge."

"I like him," said Mary Anne. "He's a gentle soul, I think."

"I'm going back to our room and do my calculus homework for about an hour, but I'm going to be ready to beat your pants off at 500 Rummy this afternoon, Christopher, so you'd better be ready to eat some crow."

"Bring it on, brother! Bring it on."

Jonathon gathered up his books and went into the bedroom. Determined to be through with his least favorite subject, social studies, by time to leave. He'd never seen to point in learning about the different branches of government, but lately, with the war going on, he'd been paying closer attention. Somebody had to pay the bills and somebody had to make sure it was done correctly. So maybe there was a need for a treasury and a place for people to take their grievances. By the time he'd read three chapters ahead and he still had an hour to go before he could leave, playing a game of rummy seemed like a good idea.

"Blast it," he said as Christopher laid down his cards yet again. "You are the luckiest guy I've ever met."

Christopher grinned. "Maybe next time, Jonathon. Don't count on it, but maybe next time."

Mary Anne came over to the sofa where her brothers had been playing. "See if you can beat me, Christopher Robin. See if you can beat me."

"Stop calling me that. You had a teddy bear too."

"True, but I didn't name him Winnie."

Jonathon left his brother and sister to the banter and knocked on Mom's bedroom door. "Mom? May I come in?" He heard the bedspread rustle and his mother's feet hit the floor.

"Yes dear. I was reading."

"I'm about to take off. Do you still want me to swing by our house?"

Mom nodded. "People are probably already wondering what's going on with us, why not give them some more grist for their rumor mill."

"I think Jennifer should be back home by four, so that'll give me time to go before I see her. Even if I meet up with her on the street our story still hangs together." He kissed his mom on the cheek. "And, yes, I'll be very careful. Oh, do you want me to stop at the store if I find the ration coupons?"

"Yes, please. Just get milk, bread and coffee. I'm sure they'll bring us more food tomorrow. We have enough for a light dinner tonight."

"It doesn't get dark until nine, so I should be back in plenty of time." He grinned and left the room.

Christopher and Mary Anne looked up from their game of Monopoly. "Where are you going, Jonathon?"

"Mom asked me to run some errands."

"Can we go?" asked Christopher, a mischievous glint in his eye.

"No, you may not go," said Jonathon, trying not to smirk.

Chapter 35

"WHY NOT?" ASKED MARY Anne.

"Safer," said Jonathon.

Before they could respond, Jonathon edged the front door open far enough to slip his body out. Once in the hallway, he stood with his back to the near wall and listened. He didn't hear anything but his own panting breath. He shrugged his shoulders up and down to relieve tension there, took a deep breath, held it, and then silently eased it out through his mouth.

Hearing no other noise in the hall, and seeing no movement, shadowy or otherwise, Jonathon headed, heel to toe up toward the stairwell. He didn't think it was a good idea to use the elevator. Too much chance of meeting other tenants.

He eased the door to the steps open and peeked up and down. Nobody he could see, so he listened for breathing or movement. Nothing. Either there was nobody around, or, if there was, that person was good at his job.

He headed down the stairs. Wait, maybe it would be better to go up to the roof and down the outside steps from there. Then he could just appear on the street as if he'd come from somewhere else. He nodded and awarded himself with a mental pat on the back.

When he reached the door to the roof, he grabbed the handle and pulled. It didn't budge. Was it locked? He didn't find any knob to twist, so it must not be a deadbolt. Nor was there a slot to insert a key. He pulled again, harder this time. Still the door wouldn't budge. He looked at the hinges and realized he was supposed to push. Warm California air flowed in toward him. He stood and listened again, but all he could hear was the sound of cars going by on the street below and the wind whispering by his ear.

Feeling more confidant, Jonathon stepped clear of the door and looked to his left. Nothing, and, more importantly, no-one there. He was about to take a step forward when he remembered to look to his right. Oh no, something was moving. He flattened himself against the doorframe, hoping whatever or whoever was there hadn't seen him.

Again, he listened and watched. Then he heard a soft "coo, coo." He looked down toward the top of the roof and breathed a shaky sigh as he saw a grey pigeon with black stripes on its wings, bob toward him.

Calm down, Jonathon, he thought, and looked around for the ladder that would take him off the roof. It was in the far left-hand corner of the building, but when he got there, he couldn't figure out which direction he was facing and the ladder only went down to adjacent building.

Jonathon sat on the edge, his feet dangling over the ladder. He looked to his left and he looked to his right. Then he looked straight down toward the ground. He didn't see the front gate and he didn't see the pool. Was he at the side of the building? He looked at his watch. He'd better hurry if he wanted to catch Jennifer at home and if he wanted to swing by his house beforehand.

He could feel panic tightening his throat and chest. That wouldn't do him any good. *Calm down, Jonathon, calm down,* he thought again, as he took yet another deep breath and shook out his arms.

Okay, he looked around for more landmarks and thought he could see the ravine he'd gone by two days ago was just off the edge of the shorter building. So that meant the pool was to his right and around a corner, which meant the front of the building was to his left and around that corner.

Going down a ladder was not his favorite thing to do, but, taking it slowly and feeling for each step, he could do it. He just wouldn't think about slipping and falling. He softly whistled "If You Wish upon a Star," from the Walt Disney movie "Pinocchio". The song always made Jonathon happy. And it worked again. He could feel the tension leaving his body. Now, if only the ladder on this lower building was in this same corner and went down to the ground, he be headed in the right direction.

Then it hit him. The building he was now on had to be part of the apartment building. So, if he was right, getting down off this part of the building would set him right where he'd been. He knew his way from there.

Almost giddy with relief, Jonathon hardly noticed he was on a ladder as he made his way down to the ground. But when he made it to the edge of the ravine, he remembered he'd still better by cautious. So, he backed up against the apartment building and stood quietly listening. Again, all he could here was street noise, rustling trees and chirping birds. He stayed close to the building anyway to give himself less chance of being noticed. When he got to the corner, he turned left and, still walking close to the building, moved along to the street.

A couple of women pushing baby carriages walked by him, chatting and laughing about something. Probably just girly stuff, Jonathon thought.

But then he wondered what Mom would be talking about if she were with them. Would she talk to them about girly stuff or would she talk them about work stuff? Probably girly stuff, he figured.

The women were walking away from where Jonathon was headed, but it seemed a good idea to go in the same direction as they, before turning left and going back toward his house. Good cover, he thought.

He walked along as if he hadn't a care in the world. As if he were where he was supposed to be at that time of day. A woman had noticed him, but only for a second before going about her business and the other people he walked past didn't even seem to see him, so he was feeling confident that he was safe, but he when he crossed to the street to head left toward his street, he noticed a man had crossed the street just behind him.

No, no-one would follow him that closely. It was too much of a give-away. Wasn't it? Even so, Jonathon turned right into one of the long alleyways and then ducked into the back entranceway of a store.

The man came by him shortly after that, headed toward the next street, but slowed as he approached it. He backtracked a few steps and looked into the entranceway down there. When he didn't see what he was apparently looking for, he turned and slowly walked back toward Jonathon's hiding place, looking in every recessed area he came to.

Jonathon turned the knob on the door behind him, relieved when the door open inward. He slipped inside and leaned against the door, listening to any noise from the alley.

Somebody stopped in front of the door and scuffled his feet back and forth, but didn't try the handle and finally left, heading back toward the way Jonathon had come.

Jonathon heard someone approaching from the interior of the store and slipped back into the alleyway. He moved more quickly down the alley and zigzagged from street to street toward his house.

His across-the-street-neighbor, Mrs. Huntsville, called to him, "Yoo Hoo, Jonathon. I was wondering where you and your family had gone. Is everything alright?"

Jonathon lifted the mailbox flap and slipped out all the mail. "Yes ma'am, we've just been busy. Hope you've been well."

"Well, I've seen all those men going in and out, so I was hoping there wasn't any trouble."

"No ma'am, we're fine. Mom just having some work done." He opened the front door, turned to wave at her, and headed inside. "Nice to see you, Mrs. Huntsville," he said and shut the door in her face. She was a nice enough old lady, but she sure was a busy body. Their block was full of them.

Still, it was nice of her to keep watch, he guessed. Just as long as she didn't blab it all over the neighborhood. Which, of course, she would.

Oh well, hopefully this whole ordeal would be over soon and they could go on with their lives.

He surveyed the living room, noting things that were out of place.

He looked at his watch and realized it was almost three thirty. He wanted to be at Jennifer's by four figuring she'd be back from choir practice by then.

He took the steps upstairs two at a time and hurried into his room to grab a couple of books to read. He was almost done with *For Whom the Bell Rings*. *Just in case we're stuck in that apartment much longer.*

He slid down the banister and was just about to slip out the front door until he saw Mrs. Huntsville still puttering in her front garden. He turned and went through the kitchen and out the maid's door again.

He stopped there suddenly wondering if anybody had told Naomi not to come until further notice. Then he thought about what their maid was doing for money if she wasn't being paid to take care of their house. "Poor Naomi," he whispered as he left the house and headed into the back yard. He turned left and walked past the garage into the formal garden with its brick walkway and beds of geraniums. Past that garden he climbed the back fence into another neighbor's yard. That neighbor worked, so Jonathon figured he could get through there unseen.

Once he got to the street he turned right and jogged toward Jennifer's house. She was just coming up her walkway to the front door as he arrived.

"Jennifer," he called, "wait for me." *She looks so beautiful,* he broke into a run and pulled her to him. He bent to kiss her, but she pushed him away.

"Jonathon, where have you been? Why haven't you called me?" She frowned and lightly swatted his arm. "I thought you'd run away or died or something."

She stepped back further and shook her head as Jonathon reached for her. "No, you don't touch me." Her eyes glittered and her voice was icy. "You still have to explain the girl at the beach."

"I will, I will." Jonathon reached his arm out. "Please, can't we just sit on your front porch and talk."

Jennifer moved to the porch and sat in the Adirondack rocking chair next to the hanging swing. She crossed her arms over her chest. "I'm listening," she said, scowling.

Even with that frown and pouting lips, Jennifer was the most beautiful girl he'd ever seen. "I wanted to call, but I wasn't allowed to. I snuck out to see you two days ago, but got caught and had to go back."

"What are you talking about?" The scowl lines smoothed about a bit. "I heard about you flirting with that girl at the beach on Sunday."

"I wasn't really flirting, just talking to her. Richard was interested in one of the other girls, so Mom invited them to share our picnic lunch."

Jennifer bunched up her lips and nodded.

"I was going to call you that afternoon, but when we got home the police were all over our house and I didn't get a chance."

Jennifer's mouth flew open. "Police? What were the police doing there?"

"Wasn't it in the papers?"

"Not that I read and my parents didn't say anything about it."

Jonathon wondered if he was supposed to tell her. He was supposed to ask for her help, so why wouldn't he tell her what happened.

Before he could say anything, Jennifer's neighbor Kurt Englemann called from the sidewalk. "Hey Jonathon, how come you're not still in jail?"

Jennifer looked at Kurt and then turned toward Jonathon with her eyebrows raised. "What's going on here?" she asked as Kurt walked up the path toward them.

"Hasn't he told you?" Kurt asked. "Mrs. Huntsville reported hearing gunshots at your house on Sunday. You know the day you were at the beach hugging Gloria."

"What's wrong with you, Kurt? Why are you trying to get me in trouble?" Jonathon turned to Jennifer. "First off, Jennifer. I wasn't hugging Gloria. Yes, I did put my arm around her shoulders to comfort her. She'd just told me something sad that happened to her."

He turned toward Kurt. "Secondly, nobody was shot at my house," Jonathon paused and growled, "ever."

"Why did Kurt say your neighbor heard gunshots?"

"Because he lies. Don't you remember how often he's been caught in lies at school?"

Jennifer lifted up her hands, palms up. "Maybe. I guess so. But why do you think he's lying now?"

198

"Because, as I just said, nobody was shot at my house."

Kurt shuffled his feet, "Well, maybe she said she saw policemen there."

Jonathon nodded at that. He turned back to Jennifer. "I was just going to tell you about that." He touched Jennifer's hand. This time she didn't pull away, but she didn't turn her palm to hold his hand. She laid her hands back in her lap and leaned a bit closer to him.

"Go on," she said.

"Could you just go home now, Kurt?"

Kurt didn't move and Jennifer said, "You may stay."

How was Jonathon to warn her against Kurt's family if he was standing right there? "Could we go for a walk? Just the two of us?"

Jennifer leaned away from Jonathon. "Why can't Kurt listen?"

"Because what I have to tell you is private. If after you listen to me, you think you can tell other people, I guess that'll be fine."

Kurt didn't move. Instead he just smiled at Jennifer, though Jonathon thought it looked more like he was smirking.

Jennifer nodded. "All right. Thanks for stopping by, Kurt I'll talk to you later."

Kurt stood there for a minute longer and then shrugged. "See you later," he muttered and headed toward the sidewalk.

Jonathon watched until Kurt cleared the bushes that separated Jennifer's yard from her neighbors'. Then he turned toward his girlfriend. At least he hoped she was still his girlfriend.

"Kurt is correct that the police were at our house when we got home. And I'm sure Mrs. Huntsville did see them, because she sees everything."

"Well what is he lying about, if that parts true?"

"Another neighbor was stabbed to death, this time in our house."

"You mean someone other than Dr. Ringwaldt?"

"Yes," Jonathon said. "By the way, did the paper say when Dr. Ringwaldt's funeral would be?"

"No. I checked on Saturday and every day since after you told me, but there's still no mention of his death." Jennifer murmured. She wiped a tear from her cheek. "He was a very nice man. Who murdered him? Do you know?" She turned toward Jonathon and touched his hand.

Jonathon shook his head and turned his hand over to encircle his fingers around her palm. "The police are investigating the murder."

"And now they're investigating the murder of Günter Schmidt, who lived behind us. He was stabbed to death as well."

"What was he doing in your house?"

"I have no idea."

Chapter 36

THEY SAT IN SILENCE for a minute, leaning closer together. Jonathon wished he could just hold her in his arms and breathe in her fresh scent. He wanted to absorb her warmth and the feel the silkiness of her hair against his cheek.

But she moved and looked up at him. "Is this why you haven't been around? Why you've skipped school?"

"Yes, we've been hiding in an apartment on the other side of Wilshire Boulevard." He kissed her nose and longed to kiss her lips, but this wasn't the right time. Maybe after he'd asked her about Kurt's family.

"I've missed you so much, Jennifer. That's why I disobeyed Mom and the police the other day. I just wanted to be near you."

She smiled at him and touched his cheek. "I've missed you too, but tell me what the police are doing to solve these murders."

Jonathon put his arms around her and told her what Dad and Richard had told him, pretending he'd hear it all from the police.

"Did they let you come see me today? Or did you sneak out, again?"

"They need your help." He held his hand up when she backed away from him. "It's nothing dangerous. I would never put you in harm's way."

"What then?"

"Well, they just wanted to know if you've seen the Engelmann's' doing anything suspicious."

"What do you mean by suspicious?" Jennifer held her index finger on each hand up signaling quotation marks. "Sneaking around with guns the way they do in movies? Or passing secret messages?"

Jonathon shook his head, "I don't really know. Maybe strange cars parked there at night or loud arguments or lots of people speaking German hanging around."

"Well, they do have a lot of German speaking men coming and going, but I assumed that's because the Englemanns usually speak German at home."

"How do you know that?"

She shrugged, "I hear them when I go to help Kurt with his English homework."

She stopped for a minute. "Come to think of it, I'm pretty sure I saw a picture of Hitler hung up in their den. Mr. Englemann was in there one time when I walked past on my way to the sunroom. He saw me looking and slammed the door in my face."

Just as Jonathon was about respond, Kurt stepped out from around the side of the house. He held a gun in his right hand pointing right at Jonathon's temple. "Do not say anything more, Jennifer. You do and I will shoot your boyfriend in the head."

He waved his left hand away from the couple. "Jennifer, you move here beside me. I don't want to hurt you."

He looked at Jonathon. "And you stay right where you are. My *vater* is coming soon. I have called him on the telephone."

"What? You think I'm going to stand here and wait with Jennifer in danger? How are you going to get rid of me and not get rid of her?" Jonathon shook his head. "You're not thinking clearly, my friend."

"I am not your friend."

"That may be true, but I'm not letting you hurt Jennifer. Let her go."

Jonathon knocked his girlfriend to the porch floor and dove off the porch landing on his shoulder and rolling to his right. He came up close to Kurt's right knee and kicked out with his leg. He heard a loud boom in his ear and heard Jennifer scream, "Mom! Call the police."

Then he felt a searing pain along his right ear. Kurt had shot him. He looked up to see Kurt ready to shoot him again.

Jonathon staggered up into a crouch and, head down, launched himself toward the boy's midsection. He felt his forehead connect with Kurt's hard abdomen and then hear him grunt as he fell to the ground. The gun discharged again, the bullet whizzing past Jonathon's head and thunking into the trunk of a palm tree in Jennifer's front yard. He sat on Kurt's chest and wrestled the gun out of his hand.

"Jennifer, go inside and call the police. Then stay inside until they get here."

"Mom's already calling them. Throw the gun toward me. I'll take it in with me."

Kurt struggled to get out from under Jonathon, but he knew he couldn't do it. Jonathon was too big.

"Give up, Kurt, you know it's over. Just wait for the good guys to come."

"We're are the good guys. Germany's the good side," he mumbled.

Jonathon's ear was stinging and he could feel blood dripping down his cheek, so he was very glad to hear approaching police sirens. And he was even gladder to see Jennifer coming out of the house carrying a first aid kit. Her mother was right behind her.

"Oh Jonathon, are you hurt badly? Mom brought rope to tie Kurt up with. The police are all most here." Jennifer hovered near him, but jumped out of the way of Kurt's grasping hand.

Mrs. Murphy grabbed hold of Kurt's arm and slipped a loop of rope over it. She tightened that and lifted up his head to slip the rest of rope behind him. Then she tightened a loop around his other arm and ran the rope down to his ankle. Soon she had him bound arm and leg. She motioned for Jonathon to get off and flipped Kurt over so she could pull him into a backward bend. "For your information, that's how you hog-tie a calf," her Texas drawl slipping out in her speech.

Jennifer ran over to Jonathon and held him close. She leaned him against her chest and went to work doctoring his ear. In between each dab with the gauze, she kissed him on the ear, until he couldn't stand it any longer. He turned to face her and pulled her on top of him. He gently pushed her head toward his and planted a kiss on her lips.

They didn't move until they heard a giggle from her mother and a harrumph from a man. Jonathon looked up and saw his father standing above them grinning like he'd never seen anything funnier.

Jonathon kissed Jennifer on the nose and said, "We'll finish this later, honey."

Chapter 37

JONATHON STOOD UP AFTER Jennifer rolled clear of him and extended his hand to her. Several policemen were slouching near the sidewalk with little smiles on their faces. Except for Jack, who had a big grin smeared across his face.

Kurt was being untied and put in handcuffs. He grimaced and snarled at Jonathon. "I'll get you yet," he said.

Jonathon bit his lip to keep from saying anything snide. "I'm sorry you feel that way," he said and turned to his dad. "What happens now?"

"Now we take you back to the apartment and wait for Kurt's father to show up. I'm sure he's been called by now."

"Yes, Kurt said he'd called him," said Jonathon.

"Let's go sit on the porch," said Jennifer.

When they were seated on the front porch, Jennifer asked, "What will happen to Kurt, Major Thomas? He's the same as age as we are."

"He did shoot Jonathon," said Mrs. Murphy.

"Yes, but he still won't get any real jail time," said Jonathon. "At least, I hope he doesn't. He's probably just been brainwashed by his parents."

Jennifer squeezed his hand.

His father said, "Well, probably they'll be kept in seclusion until the war is over so they can't cause any more harm."

"Do you think you can round up the whole gang?" asked Jennifer's mother.

"Certainly hope so," Jonathon's dad nodded. "But it depends on how willing Karl is to cooperate."

He stood up and turned to the group. "I'm sorry to have gotten you involved, but thank you for your help."

Mrs. Murphy shuddered, "Glad we could help, but I'd just as soon not be any further involved."

"I understand." Dad turned to Jennifer. "I'm afraid Jonathon won't be back in school until next week. We want to make sure the Englemann gang doesn't cause any more trouble."

Mrs. Murphy's eyes widened and Jennifer squeaked. "Are we safe here?" they asked.

Major Thomas nodded. "We'll put out a story that Jonathon was just visiting and Kurt got jealous."

Jennifer headed toward the front door. "Do I have to go to school tomorrow, Mom? I don't want to answer a lot of questions."

"We'll keep it out of the papers. The way we did with the two stabbings on our street. You should be safe." Major Thomas turned to Jonathon, "Come on, Son. I'll race you back to the apartment."

Jonathon shook Mrs. Murphy's hand and hugged Jennifer. Then he grinned and pushed his father aside. "Last one to the apartment has to do dishes for a week." He jumped off the porch and took off down the street, his dad close on his heels.

They made it to the front gate nose to nose.

"Guess we do the dishes together, Son."

"What? My big toe hit the gate before yours!"

Jonathon's grin disappeared. "Wait! I told Mom I'd pick up food if we got our coupons." He patted his pockets. "What did I do with the mail?"

"It fell on the ground while you were wrestling with Kurt." Dad smiled. "I picked up some stuff for dinner earlier."

"Thanks, but we still have to do the dishes together."

"Well, I won't be around much, so the dish washing honor will be yours by default anyway." Dad squeezed Jonathon's shoulder and held the front door open.

As they headed up the stairs, Jonathon said, "I've been thinking about my Babe Ruth card with the writing on it."

"What about it?"

"Have you guys translated it?"

"I'm not sure they've even found it yet. It's alphabetized in with the other cards, isn't it?"

"Yes sir, but I don't use the players' names. I put them in by their life-time average, if they're retired, and the active players are in a different box."

"So, he'd be up front?" Dad's forehead was wrinkled in a frown.

Jonathon nodded. "I can find it, if you let me have the box."

"I'll just tell the guys at the office."

"I'm going to get my cards back at some point, aren't I?"

Dad pulled the door to their floor ajar, stopped, listened, and then stuck his foot out into the hallway. When he didn't hear any noise, he opened the door wider and stepped into the corridor. They were in the apartment in two steps.

Jonathon exhaled a shaky breath, glad to be safe again. He assured his mother his ear wasn't going to fall off. "When's dinner? I'm starving."

His father headed out after a snack, saying, "I'll be back soon."

"Hope you find the card," said Jonathon and patted his dad's shoulder, glad he could now look him in the eye without having to tilt his head.

"Hey brother mine, we're just going for a swim before dinner," said Christopher. "Do you want to come?"

"I'll be right there."

They didn't hear from anybody until two days later, when Richard flung the front door wide open. "We gottem!"

"Who?" asked Christopher.

"How? asked Jonathon.

"Can we go home, now?" asked Mary Anne.

"Can I go back to work, now?" asked Mom.

Dad walked in and said. "Sit down everybody and we'll fill you in."

After the family was settled in the living area, Dad started. "The research group found the Ruth card right where you said it would be, Jonathon. Turns out Karl Englemann is the ring leader. At least of this group."

"Oh dear, poor Kurt," said Mom.

"What's going to happen to that family?" asked Mary Anne.

"Deported back to Germany, I'm sure," said Christopher. "Sure don't want them in our country."

"Now Christopher," said Mom, using her stern, don't-be-rude voice. "They're just misguided. Maybe they'll change their ways after they learn the truth about their country."

"Actually, the family will be kept in a Prisoner of War camp until the war is over," said Richard.

"Oh," said Dad. "You remember Helmut Jungen, don't you?"

"Is he alright?" asked Jonathon.

"Weird fellow," said Christopher.

"Scares me," said Mary Anne.

Dad smiled, but he looked sad. "Well, Jonathon, I guess you could say he's alright. I mean I only shot him in the leg when he attacked me."

"What?" Mom leapt out of her chair.

Dad held his hand up and pulled Mom into his lap. "Turns out we really hadn't flipped him."

"What's that supposed to mean?" asked Christopher.

After getting a nod of approval from Dad, Richard said, "The OSS first found out about him because he was spying for Germany."

Mary Anne nodded. "I knew he was bad."

Dad smiled. "Well, we thought we'd turned him. He agreed to spy for the U.S."

"Or so we thought," said Richard.

"Was Dr. Ringwaldt a German agent also?" Asked Jonathon, sitting up in his chair and frowning. "He was my friend."

Dad shook his head. "No, Bruno was trying to convince Helmut to help the Allies. And, yes, he was very fond of you, Jonathon." Dad smiled and said, "Anyway, thanks to your Babe Ruth card, we were able to sort this all out. Like the Englemanns, Helmut will be kept in prison until the end of the war."

Dad set Mom on her feet, stood up, and clapped his hands. "The best news of all is that we're free to go home!" said Dad.

"Right now?" chorused everybody else.

"Yep," said Richard. "Pack up."

"Wait," said Jonathon. "I have one more question."

"Ask away," said Dad.

"Did you ever figure out how Kurt knew I'd met Gloria at the beach?"

Richard nodded. "Yeah, I was worried Madge was involved somehow. She seemed like a good woman."

Dad sat back down. "Richard asked her out on a date and while they were having dinner, she apologized to him. She said Gloria had been conned by Kurt whom she knew through church functions into believing that if she helped him, he could help find her cousin Daphne."

"So, she called Kurt when she got home," said Christopher.

Richard shook his head, "No, Kurt called her."

"But how did she know that Kurt wanted to know about Jonathon?" asked Mary Anne.

"Well, she didn't really, until Kurt wanted to chat and she told him about meeting us and that Jonathon had mentioned his girlfriend Jennifer." Richard flipped his hands in the air. "The whole thing was just a coincidence."

"But the whole thing still seems a bit fishy to me," said Dad, so we're keeping an eye on her."

"Can we go home now? I really want to go home," said Mom.

"Let's go," said Dad.

Jonathon was the first one into their house and made a beeline for the stairs with Mom's and his suitcases. He was about to take the luggage upstairs when he remembered Granny was supposed to come live with them. Where should he put his suitcase? He wondered. He left the bags at the foot of the stairs and wandered into the living room. There was a telegram on the foyer floor just inside the front door. He handed it to Mom when she came in from the kitchen.

After they were all in the house, Mom opened it and wrinkled her forehead. "It's from Granny. She's on her way home." She handed the wire to Dad before moving to the sofa in front of the fireplace. "Where are we going to put her?"

Dad was reading the message again. "Uh, oh! This was delivered two days ago."

"Good lord," said Mom, standing up. "I don't have her room ready. I don't have anything ready."

Dad gave Mom a hug. "It'll be alright, Marian. We'll put her in your front room, and let the boys stay where they are."

"Plenty of room, Mom," said Richard. I've got to go into a special training session for about six months, so I won't even be here."

"Where will you be, Dad?" asked Christopher.

"I don't know quite yet, son, but they're sending me back out into the field soon."

Mom's eyes leaked tears, and she brushed them angrily off her cheek. Closest thing to a scowl Jonathon had ever seen her make crossed her face.

Later that night, Jonathon settled into his own bed with a sigh. *Now for a good night's sleep,* he hoped.

Again, the ground shook. And he was on desert land with huge fractures all around him. But there was a cactus in full bloom on his little piece of earth and across a looming chasm he could see his whole family reaching to help him and Jennifer's musical voice urged him on. "Just reach for us, Jonathon. We'll help you."

He woke up smiling, knowing he'd never have that dream again.

Study Questions

(Note to teachers. These are all complicated subjects.)

I.   Questions about U.S. enemies during WWII.
  - A. Describe the reasons for the war.
  - B. Who started it?
  - C. How long before U.S. involvement had the war been going on and where?
  - D. What was the U.S. role in the start of the war? For instance, my paternal grandfather felt that if we didn't try to understand Japanese culture better, we'd end up in a war with them. In 1915 he sent my then five-year-old father to a Japanese speaking school. Oddly enough, that may have spared him and his fellow prisoners of war even more hardship in the Philippines.

II.   Questions about wartime life in the U.S.
  - A. What effects did the war have on everyday life in the U.S.?
  - B. How did women's and children's lives change?
  - C. Who were Rosie the Riveters and what were their duties? My mother was Lockheed's first female tool & dye designer, an Army wife and mother, and an Army "brat," so the government thought she'd be a good role model. Probably didn't hurt that she was a pretty natural blonde.
  - D. Were Japanese/ and German/Americans treated any differently during the war?

III.   Questions about events leading up the war.
  - A. How were the U.S. and World economies doing before the war?
  - B. What social issues were emerging in the 1930s, 40s and 50s?

IV.   Music and other cultural changes
    A. Describe the changes to popular music, film and literature.
    B. Describe the changes to popular clothing for males and females.

Photographs

Author's mother, Priscilla Bunker Maury (in white,) about to christen a
ship representing the Rosie the Riveter organization and the government.

Author's sister, Anne,
with family friends
at the beach.

Author's mother and
brother Bill standing
at the edge of our
driveway. Shows what
the street looks like.

Author's mother, a Rosie the Riveter, and sister
collecting rubber for the war effort.

About the Author

Sarah Maury Swan was two when this photo was taken in front of the family home on Van Ness Avenue, Hollywood, CA. *Earthquakes* storyline came to her because people kept telling her to write her mother's story. Well, she didn't feel she could do that since she's not her mother. But she could add some of the family history into this story.

Many of Ms. Swan's stories have placed in the Carteret Writers' annual contest, as well as the Pamlico Writers' Group contest. When she's not writing, Sarah reviews children's books for the Children's Literature Comprehensive Database, www. clcd.com and her husband and she put on "house concerts."

Her first published novel, *Terror's Identity*, got excellent marks from the judge of the 2017 "Writer's Digest Self-Published Books Contest," children's book category. The opening chapter also came in first in the Carteret Writers 2015 Fiction category.

Her second novel, *Emily's Ride to Courage*, is garnering outstanding reviews. The first chapter placed in the 2017 Carteret Writers Children's category.

Please check her website: www.sarahmauryswanlovesbooks.com for availability. You can also find her on www.sarahsbookreflections.com where she posts blogs most Wednesdays.